PRAISE FOR *THE CASE OF WINDY LAKE*,
BOOK ONE IN THE MIGHTY MUSKRATS MYSTERY SERIES:

"These tweens are smart, curious, and resourceful."

—JEAN MENDOZA, AMERICAN INDIANS IN CHILDREN'S LITERATURE (AICL)

"The Muskrats feel like the kind of real kids that have been missing in children's books for quite some time."

—QUILL & QUIRE

"Chickadee's rez-tech savvy pairs well with her cousin Otter's bushcraft skills, and, along with Atim's brawn and brother Samuel's leadership, the four make a fine team.... [A]n Indigenous version of the Hardy Boys full of rez humor."

—KIRKUS REVIEWS

"Their makeshift fort in a rusted-out school bus has the appeal of the Boxcar Children's titular boxcar, and in fact there's overall an old-fashioned classic mystery feel along with a look at contemporary rez life in this first installment of a series."

—THE BULLETIN OF THE CENTER FOR CHILDREN'S BOOKS

"[A] smart and thought-provoking mystery for middle grade readers."

—FOREWORD REVIEWS

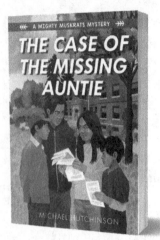

THE CASE OF THE BURGLED BUNDLE

◄◄◄ A MIGHTY MUSKRATS MYSTERY ▸▸▸
BOOK THREE

THE CASE OF THE BURGLED BUNDLE

MICHAEL HUTCHINSON

Second Story Press

Library and Archives Canada Cataloguing in Publication

Title: The case of the burgled bundle / Michael Hutchinson.
Names: Hutchinson, Michael, 1971- author.
Series: Hutchinson, Michael, 1971- Mighty Muskrats mystery ; bk. 3.
Description: Series statement: A Mighty Muskrats mystery ; book 3
Identifiers: Canadiana (print) 20200332422 | Canadiana (ebook)
    20200332430 | ISBN 9781772601664 (softcover) | ISBN
    9781772601770 (hardcover) | ISBN 9781772601671 (EPUB)
Classification: LCC PS8615.U827 C364 2020 | DDC jC813/.6—dc23

Edited by Kathryn Cole

Third printing 2021

Printed and bound in Canada

*Second Story Press gratefully acknowledges the support of the Ontario Arts
Council and the Canada Council for the Arts for our publishing program.
We acknowledge the financial support of the Government of Canada
through the Canada Book Fund.*

 ONTARIO ARTS COUNCIL
CONSEIL DES ARTS DE L'ONTARIO

 Canada Council   Conseil des Arts
for the Arts   du Canada

Funded by the Government of Canada
Financé par le gouvernement du Canada | Canadä

Published by
Second Story Press
20 Maud Street, Suite 401
Toronto, Ontario, Canada
M5V 2M5
www.secondstorypress.ca

MIX
Paper from
responsible sources
FSC® C103567

This book is dedicated to the Elders, Knowledge Keepers, teachers of skills and culture, and those older relatives who have a story for every bend in the river, oddly shaped rock, or camping spot within their traditional territory.

It is also dedicated to the Life-bearers within my own family, who have done so much to keep us all on a good path. Your work and teachings have put together a wonderful blanket that keeps us all warm and as safe as Creation's Law allows. Thank you.

CHAPTER 1

A Gathering of Crees

"Our ceremonies shouldn't be hidden. The people need them!"

The Muskrats were surprised by the touch of frustration in their grandfather's voice. Atim, Chickadee, Otter, and Samuel followed their Elder toward a large, painted teepee sitting almost in the middle of the crowded grounds of the National Assembly of Cree Peoples.

"What do you mean, Grandpa?" Chickadee held his soft, brown hand in her own. She looked up at his wrinkled face with a smile touching her pudgy, lightly freckled cheeks.

Grandpa was in his best buckskin. His long, gray hair drifted in the wind, a gnarled, wooden staff aided his walking, and the beaded bag that held his long pipe was nestled along the length of his forearm. They had just been told the handover ceremony with last year's host community, Butterfly Narrows, was happening in the huge teepee decorated with painted butterflies.

With his arm, Grandpa made a sweeping motion that took in the large crowd. "The handover is part of the welcoming ceremonies! Aren't all these folks welcome?"

"Look at all the people!" Atim, the tallest and most athletic of the Muskrats flicked the shaggy fringe of black hair out of his eyes. He was amazed. "I've never seen so many Neechies."

The other Muskrats nodded slowly, preoccupied with how many Crees—Neechies, as Atim put it—were there.

The National Assembly of Cree Peoples had attracted families from the different Nehiyew societies—from the Atikamekw Cree in Quebec to the Plains Cree living in the Rocky Mountains of Alberta—to little, old Windy Lake.

For the past few days, clusters of teepees, tents, and RVs had sprouted in every spare field and park on the reserve and in the neighboring Métis and Canadian municipality, too. Some had grown into little villages. Spread over the next seven days, the event included lessons on bushcraft, celebrations of language and culture, and competitions in canoeing, foot racing, beading, leatherwork, and other traditional activities. There was even a softball tournament with teams from across the country.

The crowd grew thicker as the Muskrats and Grandpa moved closer to the teepee. The boys sprang into action.

"Excuse us." Samuel reached up and tapped between two braids of black hair that lay over a black, leather vest.

The well-muscled man turned and looked down at Sam's smiling face. "How's it going, Haircut?"

Sam laughed and ran his fingers through his short-cropped, dark hair before waving his thumb over his shoulder. "V.I.G. coming through."

"V.I.G?" the man drawled through a smirk.

Atim stepped forward and tried to sound official. "Very Important Grandpa."

Slowly, the big guy looked past the kids at the old man. He nodded at Grandpa and stepped to the side. The four children and their V.I.G. moved forward. The Muskrats formed a phalanx around their grandfather and, as politely and quietly as possible, made their way through the crowd.

Otter studied the painted markings on the big tee-pee. "It doesn't look like it belongs to anyone from Windy Lake, Grandpa." Otter was the smallest of the Muskrats and was always dressed in a baseball cap and hand-me-downs that were too big. After his parents had died in a car accident, he had grown up with Grandpa and their late grandmother.

Grandpa's walking stick *tick-tick-tick*ed as it hit the ground. "These ceremonies were to be held in the arbor. I do not remember this being discussed at the organization meetings." The pace of the *tick*s quickened.

Chickadee noticed a middle-aged man listening intently through the tent wall to the hidden ceremony inside. Every so often, he would lean over to describe, in Cree, what he heard to an ancient woman seated in a folding chair beside him. Her silver hair was spread over a blanket wrapped around her frail shoulders. The grandmother was hungry to be a part of what was going on inside. She wasn't the only one. Other people, standing a step outside the thin walls, struggled to hear the murmur inside. They leaned, ears to canvas, hoping a whisper of wisdom would seep through. Those just a step farther away had no hope of experiencing the ceremony.

Like many teepees, the door had a wide belt along the ground that helped hold the whole structure together. Someone had built a wooden ramp, with handrails, to help those in wheelchairs over this canvas strap that ran across the bottom of the large oval entrance.

A young man with braids guarded the wooden ramp. He wore a leather vest and a ribbon shirt, a dress shirt decorated with ribbons in colors that had spiritual meaning to the wearer. He held up his hand as the Muskrats and their grandfather stepped out of the crowd.

"Sorry, sir…you are?" The twenty-something fellow lifted an eyebrow.

Grandpa stood silently as his bodyguards spoke.

"He's the head of the Windy Lake Elders Committee," Samuel asserted seriously.

"Yeah. If anyone should be inside, Grandpa should."
Atim crossed his arms.

"You can't stop *him*!" Chickadee smiled up at the
guard.

A few of the nearby Windy Lake people in the crowd
started to pay attention.

With an amused grin growing, the young man looked
at each of the Muskrats in turn. Eventually, he looked
down at Otter. "You got anything to say?"

Otter stepped aside so his Elder could be seen fully.
He motioned to the long, fringed bag that held the old
man's pipe. "My grandpa carries a pipe."

Those words worked. The young man stepped aside.

With a proud smile, Grandpa nodded at his grandchildren and made his way across the ramp.

"Only one helper per Pipe Carrier." Again, the young
man held up his hand to stop the Muskrats.

They looked at one another, but there was no question
who was going. They gave Otter a nod.

Growing up with his grandparents made Otter the
most familiar with ceremony. He bounced up the ramp to
help Grandpa step through the canvas opening and over
the gap between the outside and inside ramps.

Atim, Chickadee, and Samuel watched the two enter
the teepee. After they entered, the guard closed the door
flap behind them before resuming his post.

Chickadee noticed Samuel watching the young man. "Don't!" she whispered the warning to her skinny cousin. "He might think you're burning him."

Sam smiled and shrugged.

She looked to Atim for help, but he just lifted a shoulder and chuckled.

"Why isn't the ceremony happening out in the open?" Sam turned to the young man, trying to sound more curious than challenging.

"Colonialism!" The guard spat the word. "We have to protect our ceremonies…for when the city people try to take away the rest of our culture!"

"You mean, even now?" Samuel squinted into the setting sun as he looked up at the ramp guard.

A glimmer of scorn flitted across the young man's face before it settled on amused pity. "Of course, even now! They want to break our connection to the land. Our ceremonies keep that connection and keep us centered."

"But First Nation ceremonies are not against the law now," Atim said.

"Doesn't matter! Laws can change." The young man shook his head. "We have to keep the ceremonies hidden. They can't be taken away by the city people or sold by the weak. At Butterfly Narrows the ceremony is strong and it's strong because we protect it."

"But look at all these people." Chickadee spoke softly as she scanned the crowd. "Like you said, some First

Nations had their ceremony taken away from them. But now, they're hungry for their ancestors' teachings."

The guard studied the people around him, his eyes squinting. They fell on the old lady in the foldout chair and her translator, listening so intently to the ceremony inside.

"I guess…." He paused, uncertain.

"Butterfly Narrows could help everyone whose connection was damaged due to colonialism." Chickadee's smile beamed. Samuel and Atim quietly watched Chickadee's line of thinking play out.

The guard's imagination explored the idea but got snagged on the lessons of his childhood. He shook his head. "Some people need to be protectors. That's Butterfly Narrows. Others will have to be teachers." He nodded to confirm his firm stance, then turned back to Chickadee. "Maybe *you* should be a teacher. You made me think…for a minute there."

Sam stuck out his hand. "That's my cousin, Chickadee. My name's Samuel, but most people call me Sam."

Slowly, the young man took his hand in a firm grip. "Hi, Sam. I'm Casey."

Samuel gestured toward his brother. "This is my brother, Atim. We're from Windy Lake."

Casey nodded at the wide expanse of water behind the arbor grounds. "It's a nice place. Beautiful lake."

"It was our grandpa and our cousin Otter who went

in the teepee." Chickadee lip-pointed toward the tent, keeping her hands firmly buried in the front pocket of her favorite hoodie.

"Always nice to meet Cree people from far away." Atim nodded to their new acquaintance.

"Yes! I'm always surprised at how different we Cree can be!" Casey's smile seemed to appear from nowhere.

"Grandpa says, you are the land you live on. And the Cree people are spread across some pretty different landscapes." Chickadee chuckled.

"The Mohawk say there's a Cree behind every tree," Atim said with mock authority.

"Let's not tell them what we're doing behind there." Sam smirked, and they all laughed.

A head popped out through the teepee's canvas door, and Casey was summoned.

As he crossed the ramp, Casey called over his shoulder. "You kids *must* be Neechies. You're funny!"

The steady beat of a drum began from inside the teepee. It was quickly joined by a chorus of male voices singing in Cree.

"I think I need an Indian taco." Atim rubbed his tummy. "How much money we got?"

Chickadee and Sam groaned.

Sam lifted his eyebrows. "The ceremony *will* take a while."

Chickadee tossed her long, black hair over her

shoulder and waved for Atim to follow her. "Okay. I have some money. Come on, Goofy."

The trio made their way through the crowd to the Windy Lake arbor's parking lot where a couple of food trucks had set up. Picnic tables had been scattered nearby to make a temporary food court.

After purchasing an Indian taco, Chickadee and her cousins sat down to share the mess of bannock, taco meat, salsa, cheese, and lettuce. Filtered through the crowd and trees, the drumming and singing from inside the teepee were fainter here.

"Indian tacos," Atim said joyfully, as salsa dripped from the corner of his mouth. "I love Indian tacos. They're my favorite form of cultural appropriation." He returned to shoveling the food into his mouth.

Chickadee and Sam giggled.

Suddenly, Chickadee stopped. "Oh, great. Look who's coming." She stared down at the table.

Chickadee's body language told Sam everything. He didn't bother to look. Every community has its share of bad apples, sometimes families of them, and Windy Lake was no different.

A large fifteen-year-old, dark circles painted around her eyes and dressed entirely in black, sneered as she walked up to them. "If it isn't the Swamp Rodents!" she hissed through a mouthful of crooked teeth.

Her name was Pearl. She came from a tough family

and had managed to argue her way to leadership of a group of siblings and cousins.

"Hey, Pearl." Her derision never seemed to touch Atim.

Chickadee continued staring at the table, waiting for the bullies to leave.

"Good to see you all." Sam turned around and smirked. "Y'all enjoying the National Assembly of Cree Peoples?"

Pearl's second-in-command, Bug, loved to brag. He was too thin and too dirty. "Ohhh, yeah. Nothing easier to break into than a tent. And there's lots of tents." He gleefully slapped his filthy jeans and flashed a grin that was missing a chicklet or two. A couple of the others in the crew smiled and grunted in agreement.

"You guys are stealing from the guests?!" Atim couldn't hide the disgust in his voice.

"Quit telling stories!" Pearl slapped Bug on the back of the head. "Don't tell these goody-goodies stuff like that! They'll believe you, then run and tell their cop uncle."

Pearl laughed and waved off her minion's comment. "Bug was just kidding around."

Bug rubbed the back of his head and mumbled under his breath, "Ol' Snaggletooth…."

Pearl heard him and gave him another slap. She had always been sensitive about her poorly aligned teeth. Her family had been fighting Indigenous Affairs for braces for as long as they all could remember. Pearl bragged that she had become used to the pain in her mouth caused by teeth that grew in sideways. Bug knew he could get under her skin by calling her Snaggletooth.

Pearl looked back at Sam. "We've just been people watching. Lots of people from all over."

"Yeah, no doubt." Sam's voice was insincere.

Pearl turned to leave. "Let the Swamp Rats eat their swamp food." Her crew followed.

Once they were out of earshot, Chickadee hissed. "She's been mean for such a long time!"

"Are they really stealing from the visitors who came to the Assembly? Don't they care what people say about Windy Lake?" Atim shook his head, disappointed.

"I suspect they don't." Sam tightened his lips. "And we may have just been given our latest case."

The Muskrats watched as Pearl and her minions pushed their way through the crowd.

The drums inside the teepee were suddenly silent.

CHAPTER 2
Lessons at Lunch

"It was tense!" Otter shouted to a rising sun in a cloudless sky.

It wasn't until the next morning that the Muskrats could reunite.

"Tense? Never heard of a tense ceremony." Chickadee raised her eyebrows as she walked with her cousins to volunteer for the National Assembly of Cree Peoples.

"It was sooo weird. When we first got in, Grandpa tried to be funny and he made a joke. He told the head Elder from Butterfly Narrows about having to answer a question before crossing the bridge. Something about the air-speed velocity of an unladen swallow."

"A swallow of what?" Atim scratched his head.

"Of bird." Sam gave his brother a push. "A swallow is a bird."

"Well…." Otter squinted. "I think it made the Butterfly Narrows Elder mad. He…*harrumphed*." Otter demonstrated with an exaggerated frowning face, and Chickadee giggled.

"Yeesh! That's not good." Atim grimaced. He kicked a walnut-sized stone farther down the road. It rolled to a stop ahead of the group.

Sam pinched his chin as he thought. Walking by, he kicked Atim's rock. The misshapen orb erratically bounced its way through the gravel. "We still have a week to go until the end of the Assembly. Hopefully, Grandpa will find a way to calm the waves."

"I don't know. That Elder from Butterfly Narrows looks like a toad. I could see him holding a grudge." Otter stuck out his tongue and stretched his mouth into a frog-like frown. "He doesn't seem like a happy guy."

His cousins laughed.

"Grandpa will fix it." Chickadee sounded certain.

She got a *Mhmm* from two of the boys. The other sent the rock spinning farther down the road.

"We better hurry up or we'll be late. We don't want to get Denice mad." Atim jogged up to the rock and gave it a kick, then slowed to a walk. Their older cousin Denice was in her twenties and a rising voice in the community. Her reputation for straight talk and hard work was spreading, but her younger cousins knew, if crossed, she could be a tough taskmaster.

"She said we'd have to make seven hundred sand-wiches." Chickadee's eyes got big above her round cheeks.

"That's a lot of baloney!" Samuel said with exaggerated incredulity. They all burst out laughing.

"There's Klik for the fancy people," Otter quipped. Another round of chuckles followed.

"Where exactly is the V.I.P. section in the Windy Lake School gymnasium?" Chickadee sounded concerned. The boys snickered.

"Yeah. It's not a very fancy place," Atim guffawed. No one else laughed.

Crickets chirped. A light breeze blew some dust off the road.

"You killed it!" Sam threw his hands in the air.

"Yep." Chickadee slapped Atim on the shoulder. "Killed it!"

Atim mimicked a big baby as he waved his arms and staggered down the road. "I'm funnnyyy!" he screamed in a high-pitched whine.

The rest of the pack howled and gave chase. They all began to skip, jog, and lope down the gravel road.

★

The Windy Lake School looked like a forgotten, but well-used, toy. The yearly funding shortfalls from the Department of Indigenous Affairs plus decades of pounding from children's footfalls had beaten the building into submission. The large gymnasium was a concrete hulk that held one corner of the badly bruised school in its brick teeth.

The Muskrats sauntered into the bastion of learning like royalty, unhindered. It was easy when the halls were empty. Since the school officials wanted to save money on the weekends, four out of every five lights were dark.

The gym was drab and empty. Concrete floors, ancient bleachers, and a ceiling that appeared to be covered in fluffy asbestos didn't give it a healthy feel.

"Denice is probably in the kitchen." Samuel pointed toward a door along the brick wall. Beside the doorway, a large service window for over-the-counter transactions was covered by roll-up aluminum slats. Running, pushing, and shoving, the Muskrats fought to see who would be first through the door. They burst into the kitchen.

"You just showing up now?" Their older cousin Denice smacked her hands together, and a cloud of flour exploded around her head. "There's bannock already in the oven."

"What can we do?" Otter's eyes grew wide as he pointed out a huge stack of juice boxes to his cousins.

"We got hundreds of people showing up soon, and you could still play a game of floor hockey in that gym.

Our family is in charge of lunch. We need tables, chairs, and…look, use those big rolls of paper as tablecloths." Their older cousin pointed with globs of dough stuck to her fingers.

Atim gave Denice a half-hug. "Do we have anything I could eat now?" It had been almost forty minutes since Atim had eaten.

"Work first. The aunties will be here soon." Denice used her tough voice, then quickly returned her attention to rolling out the bannock dough.

The oldest Muskrat's mouth opened, closed, then opened again. Atim held up a finger, was about to speak, but then thought better of it. On his way out of the kitchen, he grabbed a juice box.

For the rest of the morning, they all worked hard to prepare the room for the hundreds of Cree people that would soon arrive. Lunch would consist of a sandwich washed down with juice, followed by a packet of cookies. Of course, bannock, berries, and tea would be available for the Elders. The Muskrats set up tables, flung out chairs, and rolled out at least a quarter mile of paper tablecloths. They could hear the aunties, Denice, and a few older cousins cackle and tease each other from the kitchen.

Just before noon, people started to show up. Chickadee and the boys helped them get to where they wanted to go, pointed out the gym's now-open service window, and began to clean up after the crowd had eaten and left.

"Hey, Grandpa!" Chickadee called as she cleared a table of paper plates, juice boxes, and cookie wrappers. The Muskrats' Elder had just walked in through the double doorway. Since last night, he had switched his walking stick for a cane, and his regalia for his second-best town clothes. He was walking along the wall to the kitchen door.

"Hey, my Muskrats. Are you doing good deeds?"

"Yes!" the four young sleuths yelled.

"Then get back to work!" Grandpa waved his hand at the tables. "Come to me when you're done. I want to see my daughters."

"I bet they'll talk about what happened last night," Sam said quietly as he studied the door to the kitchen.

"The tension between the Elders?" Otter's voice was grave as he filled a black garbage bag with trash.

Samuel nodded.

Atim loudly tore the paper tablecloth off one of the tables. "We only have to take this stuff off and we're done. We'll have to do this all again tomorrow, so we can leave the tables and chairs."

"This was pretty fun!" Chickadee smiled. "Reminded me of the Spence Street BBQ we volunteered for in the city."

"Feels good to help out." Otter was unsuccessfully trying to let go of a sticky napkin.

His cousins enjoyed watching him wave his hand in the air. The napkin rustled rebelliously as Otter flailed.

"Probably, someone's sticky boogers." Atim sniffled, long and loud, after he said it.

Sam and Chickadee burst into laughter as Otter groaned and pulled the clinging napkin off his hand.

It didn't take the Muskrats long to clean the tables down to their boards once they focused on finishing the task.

"Okay, I want to hear what Grandpa has to say." Sam led the charge toward the kitchen door. This time, the cousins snuck in quietly, so as not to disturb any conversations in midstream.

"I forgot my own lesson! And now…this may be too big for me to fix." Grandpa was sitting on a stool.

The aunties' efforts were split between cleaning up from the last meal and preparing for the next one.

"What lesson, Grandpa?" Samuel blurted it out and immediately regretted it. Denice and his aunties smiled but shook their heads. His family preferred seekers to find their own trail. Questions can be selfish and direct, but everyone knew Sam couldn't help himself. It was one of the reasons he was occasionally labeled "City."

The Muskrats were a little awestruck that this time, Grandpa was the one seeking answers.

"The lesson that you are the land you live on. The Cree people have many different histories with the Europeans, and then the Canadians…."

Grandpa stopped, seemingly, mid-sentence. Samuel

bit his tongue. His Elder often had long pauses as he collected his thoughts, but Sam's desire to have his grandfather explain more almost burst from his chest like an alien baby.

The old man, slowly, took a sip of tea while the other Muskrats giggled as they watched Sam squirm.

Grandpa inhaled, paused, and then began to explain. "Here in Windy Lake, we're near an intersection of rivers. Our lands have always been desired. Being near a crossing, our history is one of meeting strangers, but in the case of the city people, they wanted to take control. That's why we have five churches on our little reserve. That's why we had to rediscover our ceremony grounds." Grandpa took another pause.

Denice motioned to Chickadee and the teapot. Chickadee took the tea and went over to her grandfather. He held out his cup as she drew near. The aunties carried out their work quietly.

"At Butterfly Narrows, they are in the far north at the beginning of a river, in a bit of a valley. Their lands are good to them, but they are not as valuable to the city people and their economy. And so, the Butterfly Narrows relationship with them is one of neglect…except when the Settlers wanted to send police or take something away, like their ceremonies or their children. The lands of Butterfly Narrows have taught them to hold tightly to what they have, to protect what they haven't yet lost."

Grandpa shook his head and threw up his hands, obviously disappointed in himself. "And I acted as if my lands' teachings were the only ones." He gently slapped his knee.

With sympathetic eyes, Denice walked up to Grandpa and gave him a hug. After the silent embrace, Grandpa looked down as he wiped away a lone drop.

The Muskrats gathered around him. The aunties all stopped what they were doing and smiled at their father.

"Is that why different First Nations have different kinds of treaties, Grandpa?" Samuel asked, trying to sound nonchalant.

Everyone giggled. Their oldest auntie rolled her eyes.

Grandpa reached out and ruffled his curious grandson's short, black hair. "Yes, different treaties, from different lands and their histories. Out East, they have treaties that are hundreds of years old; our treaty was made just as Canada was being born. And now, some First Nations in British Columbia and the territories are just discussing treaties with Canada! Canada is a big place, and it's taken hundreds of years for the city people to be able to have influence over all of it."

"I read our treaty once." Atim pushed the hair out of his eyes as he spoke.

"Well, that's a signed treaty; that's the Crown's side of treaty. In our legal system we 'make' treaties. Our side of the treaty is found in the oral histories of our families and the memory bundles that mark that day."

"Memory bundles?" Sam prodded.

"Well…you must always remember, nations make treaties, treaties do not make nations. Canada made treaty with First Nations because they were already nations, who had control of the land. Treaty starts with knowing that you are part of something bigger than you." Grandpa poked Sam just above his heart. "You are Sam, your mother's son, but you are also Sam from Windy Lake. And you are also Sam from the Cree Nation."

Grandpa held out his cup. But when Chickadee went to fill it, he changed his mind and waved her off. Her Elder asked for a glass of water instead—he was worried that more caffeine would make him want to pee.

Sam had no idea what Grandpa's previous comment had to do with memory bundles. The lack of closure was like an itch in his brain.

Eventually, Grandpa began to fill in the blanks. "Carrying a bundle is a big job. It is like being in charge of a memory, a memory the whole nation must remember. It's a duty to the people. When something big happens, like the making of a treaty, the people may call for a trusted person or family to make a bundle. Then the Elders sharpen and hone the stories and protocols that go with it."

Grandpa paused again. He stared at a spot on the floor for a while.

Sam's leg began to bounce. He rubbed the back of his

neck and took a deep breath. He inhaled and was about to speak. Otter poked his ribs. Sam jumped and pulled away.

Grandpa didn't seem to notice. He began to speak once again.

"The keeper of the bundle is also the keeper of the stories that go with the bundle. Keepers don't own the stories, but they must steward them through history. Tell them in the same way each time, so the next generation can be given that memory. Undamaged. Unforgotten."

"Don't you have a friend who is a treaty Bundle Holder?" one of the aunties asked her father.

"Yes, Leon Shining Deer. I've known him and his wife for years. They're good people. Wherever he goes, he always speaks about the unity the Treaty 12 bundle creates."

"Do you think that might be helpful here?" The auntie arched an eyebrow as she asked.

Grandpa sat up like he'd been hit by lightning. He slapped his knee hard enough to make a smack. "You know, I haven't seen him since your mother's funeral! I didn't even ask him if he was coming to the Assembly." Grandpa snatched his cane and hopped off the stool. "I'm going to call him now! Thank you, my daughters!"

As he left, Grandpa gave all the aunties a kiss on the cheek. Then he took off as fast as he could to call his friend from his home phone.

"You boys, go with him." Denice waved the boys out of the room.

Atim, Sam, and Otter were happy to go and they quickly caught up to their Elder.

The aunties laughed once the boys were out of earshot. "Those men! It can take a while, but they usually figure things out." The auntie who'd reminded Grandpa of his friend chuckled.

"I've never seen Grandpa so disappointed in himself." Chickadee tried to sound mildly interested, but her voice betrayed her surprise. She picked up a cloth to help dry dishes.

"He's getting older." An auntie sighed as she dried a teacup with a threadbare rag. "There is a reason that children and Elders are put beside each other on the Circle of Life."

"I remember their long talks at the kitchen table," a younger auntie said thoughtfully, as she wiped the counter.

The oldest auntie nodded and pursed her lips as her tired eyes met Chickadee's. "When he was in trouble, your grandfather always went to Mum to listen to what she thought. Now that she is gone, he comes to us."

CHAPTER 3

A Love Story

"It was the bundle that brought us together! Our love started long before we were married." Mrs. Shining Deer clung to her husband's arm.

Elder Leon Shining Deer, the Bundle Holder, had already been on his way to Windy Lake when Grandpa called. The couple had arrived later that afternoon. They were now sitting at Grandpa's scarred, wooden kitchen table, drinking tea. They hadn't seen the Muskrats since their grandmother's funeral, when they were much smaller.

Chickadee and the boys had been sent to Grandpa's to help with his visitors.

"Was it a love story, Mrs. Shining Deer?" Chickadee beamed as she filled the Cree woman's teacup. The Shining Deers were an attractive older couple, both tall, although he was slightly taller. Their long, silver hair was fanned across their shoulders, their shirts white and crisp. The turquois barrette she wore matched the turquois bolo tie that hung from Elder Leon's collar.

"You can call me Aunt Dee, dears." Her eyes twinkled as she grinned. "And, it was exactly that; a love story. I watched Leon work with my father for many years." She gave her husband a playful shove. "I watched him grow from a promising young man into a good, old one."

Elder Shining Deer's smooth, booming voice took over the story. "I was her father's fire-tender, and then his apprentice. He was a great man. A good teacher. But it was *his* father, my lovely wife's grandfather, who made Treaty 12 with the Crown." Elder Shining Deer smiled down at his better half.

Chickadee joined Otter and leaned on the kitchen counter to whisper in his ear. "Aren't they cute?"

Otter shrugged. "Seems like they're really in love," he whispered back.

"I want to hear more about the bundle." Sam pulled up at the counter and hooked a thumb in Atim's direction. "He come out of the fridge yet?"

Chickadee covered her mouth, giggled, and shook her head.

Only Atim's hind end could be seen. The rest of him was buried in a paint-chipped, brown refrigerator. From the sound and struggle, he was trying to slap something together from his grandfather's leftovers. Eventually, he emerged with a look of triumph on his face. Atim held up a soggy mess on a plate: two pieces of bread were but garnish to the chunky, multi-brown goo swimming with lumps of green that came up for air here and there.

"It's a rabbit stew and pickle sandwich. Could be the first ever."

"Something to brag about to your grandkids, I'm sure," Samuel snickered at his older brother. "If you live...."

"Shhh!" Chickadee elbowed Sam and gave Atim a stern look. She nodded toward the Elders.

Atim shook his head at the lack of appreciation for his new culinary invention, then wandered off to the living room with his plate.

"I think my dad always wanted a boy, but he got me instead." Aunt Dee laughed. "He was very traditional. He hated TV. Hated money too. Lived his life that way." Her eyes dipped into the past and she smiled warmly. "When my father knew he was nearing his final journey, he approached Leon and asked him what his intentions were. Did he plan on marrying me?"

"Of course, I told him." Elder Shining Deer chuckled and looked at his wife. "I had fallen in love with his daughter long before. We married before he passed on."

"My dad was so devoted to ceremony, so devoted to the teachings and his responsibilities toward the bundle." A bit of sadness crept into Aunt Dee's voice as she spoke. "Although, it is always given to a man to carry the treaty bundle, my dad said he wanted both of us to take care of it. He made us promise we would always be honorable to each other, and to the teachings of the bundle."

The older couple looked into each other's eyes and smiled. It was obvious they had told their love story before.

Elder Leon put a hand on his knee and shook his head, remembering harder days in the past. "The bundle can be a bit of a burden, so I am lucky to have a wife who values the old ways. I couldn't have carried the responsibility for so long if wasn't for her." He took her hand.

Aunt Dee kissed the soft, brown fingers entwined in hers. "We carried it together," she said, her voice sincere.

"Why is it such a burden?" Samuel asked Elder Leon. Grandpa gave his grandson a quick stare over his shoulder. With a look, Sam was warned not to be pushy.

Grandpa turned back to his old friend and smiled. "Samuel is a little question box. He can be like a dog with a bone, sometimes."

"So, I better answer him is what you're saying?" Elder Leon laughed, leaning back in his chair. "Don't want him to bite me."

The two old men chuckled until they slowed to a stop. They took a sip of their tea.

Elder Leon leaned forward onto the kitchen table and looked Sam over. "Taking care of the bundle is a responsibility that was given to me by Dee's father, but it really belongs to the people of Treaty 12. The bundle is their side of the treaty, but only when it is combined with the stories that go with it."

"But why do you say that it's a burden? Doesn't it make you, kind of, First Nation famous?" Sam shrugged and smiled.

Grandpa fidgeted in his chair but didn't turn around.

Aunt Dee answered for her husband. "I am a teacher at the school in our community, and I explain it like this. Imagine that an important, historic event happened in a town, and they built a library and community center to celebrate. For those teachings to live and really soak into the people's lives, the caretaker of the library would have to bring people together on important dates, they would have to educate people about the event they're honoring, and they would need people to come in and be a part of the center."

Aunt Dee looked at her husband. He supported her with a quick nod. "I tell my students; First Nations do not focus on buildings. Our important places are our camps, our fishing spots, our powwow grounds, and where rivers meet. Some of these places are where our communities are now. So, Leon and I, we must move our library around, but in each place…." She looked up at her husband. He took over the story with his low rumble.

"We do our best to bring the bundle to every community that invites us. And when we go, we must bring the people together. We have to feed them as part of the welcome for the bundle. And, when it is time to rewrap the bundle, we must tell the stories in the exact same way we have told them before. That takes four days. I carry a memory for the people."

"But what's...?" Sam pinched his chin, thoughtfully.

"That's enough questions." Grandpa turned in his chair.

Samuel nodded at his grandfather.

Elder Leon chuckled. "It's okay to ask questions. But save some for later. Better yet, I'll introduce you to our grandson, Brandon. He stayed at the camp to set it up. He is learning what it means to hold the bundle. He can answer all your questions."

Chickadee took the break in the conversation to fill up the adults' teacups.

After thanking Chickadee, Elder Leon reached across the table and squeezed his friend's forearm.

"I understand things haven't all been smooth at the Assembly."

Grandpa shook his head. "No, Leon, they haven't. Leave it to me to mess things up." The Muskrats' grandfather related how his attempt to be funny fell flat, angered the Elder from Butterfly Narrows, and caused some hurt feelings that seemed to ripple through the entire gathering.

"You were teasing, not just being funny?" Elder Leon probed his friend.

Grandpa cringed, then sighed. "Yes, you know me. I was trying to be funny, but there was a point hidden inside."

Elder Leon nodded and took a sip of tea. "That's how us Cree do it. We tease to soften the blow. That's why we only tease those we care about."

Otter stepped behind his grandfather, put a hand on his shoulder, and asked one of his rare questions. "Why do we do that, Grandpa? Why are Cree people so…tease-y?"

Leaning on the kitchen table, Grandpa looked over his shoulder as he spoke. "Because winter is so harsh, my son."

Elder Leon laughed and pointed at his old friend in agreement.

"You are the land you live on, are you not?" Grandpa raised the eyebrow closest to Otter.

"Yeah," Otter answered.

"Winter on Cree lands is very harsh. Our summers are spent preparing for the winter's darkness," Grandpa continued. "Winter was so great a challenge, that no individual could survive it. Only as a family could people make it through the long, dark nights of the cold season. This is one reason we honor our ancestors. And why the family is the building block of our nation, not the individual." Grandpa's hand moved to emphasize his words.

Elder Leon met Otter's eye, he smirked, and interrupted Grandpa's thought. "Long story short; if you got kicked out of the wigwam for being a jerk, there is a good chance you'd freeze to death."

Otter's eyes got big. "Ever deadly!"

Everyone chuckled.

Aunt Dee suppressed her giggles as she spoke. "But if you tease, it softens the blow...even if you are saying something hard."

Samuel jumped in. "I guess teasing would also give warriors more options to react to a comment than just being offended...and then fighting."

"It was important to be gentle in all things." Aunt Dee nodded, seriously. "It was a great compliment to be called a 'gentle man.'" She looked at her husband. "Remember old Bruce's funeral?"

Elder Leon nodded.

She paused in thought and looked out the kitchen window. "Old Bruce was a soldier, but the greatest thing they said about him was that he was a gentle man."

"You mean a gentleman, like someone who is polite?" Chickadee's brown brow furrowed as she asked.

Aunt Dee grinned, and shook her head. "No, it's more than that. I mean, he was a man who walked lightly on the earth. He was a hunter who only took what he needed. Who was always careful, kind, and honorable when harvesting an animal. He always spoke softly, and only when he had something valuable to say."

Elder Leon looked from his wife to the Muskrats. "To

be gentle, you have to be careful, especially when talking to others…or about others. That's why a good man's word was so valuable in the old days. You knew he was careful to give it."

Chickadee looked at Elder Leon with her big, brown eyes. "You're saying, sticks and stones may not break bones, but they can hurt hearts and poke pride…and that could get you kicked out of the wigwam?"

"Yes, and its c-c-cold outside when it's minus forty degrees." Elder Leon held himself as he pretended to shiver.

They all laughed.

The Elder nodded with appreciation at Chickadee's understanding before he spoke. "There was no paper in the old days, so a man's word was his contract. It was his flag. Our people loved someone who had a way with words, a good storyteller, a good teacher. A good person, a gentle person, knows what you say is important because, truth or lie, it reflects your heart."

Grandpa shook his head. "I forgot that when I was teasing about the hidden ceremony." His disappointment in himself was obvious. "I wasn't careful with my words. I acted as if the teachings in my lands were more important than the lessons the Elders of Butterfly Narrows were taught by their lands. I let my pride get the better of me."

"Do not be so hard on yourself, my friend." Elder Leon reached across the table and squeezed his friend's arm. "A misstep is the worst that you are guilty of…that and telling a bad joke." The old men chuckled between themselves.

"Grandpa hoped the bundle would help bring us all—the whole Assembly—together." Samuel sounded hopeful.

"It can. It will!" Elder Leon hit the table with conviction. "Tonight, we'll have the welcome ceremony. Welcome the bundle to Windy Lake, make it comfortable. Tomorrow morning, we'll begin the opening and the storytelling. We'll feel its power soon."

Aunt Dee hugged his arm tightly and smiled.

"We'll need to get this all started and make sure the people are there." Elder Leon looked thoughtful.

"Can we come, Grandpa?" Chickadee came up behind her grandfather, as he sat in his chair, and gave him a hug.

He tapped her hands and chuckled. "Of course, little one. You can all help fix Grandpa's mess."

Aunt Dee raised an eyebrow at the Muskrats. "It sounds like you guys are volunteering to help with the ceremony."

Chickadee clapped. "Can we?"

Aunt Dee nodded.

"I'll help." Otter saluted with a couple of fingers.

Samuel looked at his feet. Growing up in the city, he and his brother did not have as much experience with ceremony as Chickadee and Otter. He felt Otter's elbow in his ribs and looked up to see Elder Leon looking back at him.

Samuel smiled weakly. "Always...happy to learn... uh...more."

Just then Atim walked into the kitchen with his empty plate.

"You too?" Elder Leon asked him.

Atim looked at the other Muskrats. Their faces didn't seem too concerned. He shrugged as he put his plate in the kitchen sink. "Me too."

Aunt Dee smacked her hands together. "Good. We always need volunteers to make things go smooth."

Grandpa turned in his chair and smiled at the four children.

Mrs. Shining Deer motioned toward the Muskrats. "Their first volunteer task could be to go to our camp and tell Brandon to start preparing for the ceremony."

The young investigators nodded eagerly.

Grandpa lip-pointed at his friend. "I'll take Leon and go speak to the organization committee...tell them about the new plans. You Muskrats can meet us at the arbor grounds later."

Grandpa's door creaked loudly as his grandchildren took off, eager to pursue their next task. The Elders chuckled between themselves as four dusty clouds raced down the gravel road.

CHAPTER 4
The Bundle Holder's Apprentice

"We are all treaty people, Canadians too. Everyone benefits from our treaty."

Brandon Shining Deer was telling the Muskrats about his training as his grandfather's apprentice. He was as attractive as his grandparents, in his late-twenties, and looked at ease as he finished setting up his family's camp. His raven-black hair hung in two long braids that lay across the front of his well-worn Metallica T-shirt.

The Muskrats had been wanting to explore one of the guest camps since people started arriving. Although, the RVs, tents, and teepees had put a new face on familiar areas of Windy Lake, it didn't take them long to find the Shining Deer camp. The chrome profile of a majestic, antlered deer graced the grill of a large RV, and beside it was a small teepee. A small, blue car also sat on the lot.

The Muskrats sat around a picnic table slapped together out of thick, rough boards, painted brown. The Windy Lake band staff had built a bunch of them and had scattered them throughout the camps.

Otter felt like he'd found a kindred spirit in Brandon. "Our grandpa says that our people never fought Canada. The treaties we signed—I mean, the treaties we *made*—were peace and friendship treaties. They are about sharing the land."

"That's true of my people too. My people believed everyone would share the bounty of the Treaty 12 area equally. A big part of learning about the treaty bundle is learning the oral history that goes with it." Brandon finished his last bit of camp work and pulled up a folding chair.

Atim scratched his head. "Is it weird that we're all Cree, and Brandon is talking about his land, and Otter is talking about his land?"

"Not any weirder than it is for an Albertan to love his lands, and a Manitoban to say his heart belongs in Manitoba. They're both Canadians, right? But people come to love the lands they know."

With his leg bouncing, Samuel had been waiting for his turn to ask a question. "How do you keep telling the stories the same way? How do you learn them all?"

"Well, first, I'm just an apprentice. It'll be years before I'm in charge of the bundle. But Grandfather tells the stories often, sometimes at events we take the bundle to and sometimes to visitors that drop by. Of course, I am always there to listen. I have been since I was a child." Brandon laughed to himself and shook his head. "When I was a little kid, I had to recite the easier bits of the stories for my Elders' entertainment—for visitors, passing vacuum salesmen—pretty much everybody. And I can assure you, if they knew the stories, I was corrected if I missed the slightest word."

Otter raised his eyebrows, impressed. "I've always wondered how musicians can play a whole concert and not miss a note."

"Yes. But it's easier to memorize something if it all fits together." Brandon nodded at Otter. "The bundle is more than just the history I've learned." He opened his palms like he was opening the bundle. "I've seen it so many times. When we open the bundle in the Treaty 12 area, it inspires people to tell their family's history. They share the stories that were passed down to them from their ancestors. Could be that their great-great-grandparent was at the negotiation table or maybe just there as a witness, or maybe their dad took them there. Who knows? But there are many different stories and all of these are part of the history surrounding the treaty. In some ways, they are the First Nations' side of the treaty. They represent our understanding of the treaty contract, just as the bundle does."

"So, you couldn't just go to one place to get the oral history on Treaty 12?" Samuel's brow furrowed as he asked.

"No. My grandfather would be a good place to start. But to get the whole story, you'd need to speak to families that were there and even some that weren't there. In many cases, those families that did not support the treaty relationship with Canada just didn't show up at the meetings with the treaty commissioner. That's part of the history of the treaty too." Brandon shrugged and got out of his chair. "So, are you guys going to help me prepare for the ceremony?" The Bundle Holder's apprentice looked around at the Muskrats.

They all nodded with eager smiles.

"Okay. Each bundle has different rules and protocols that go with it. There are different ceremonies and even different colors and foods that are linked to the stories that go with the bundle. Do you know who is making the meal for the Assembly this evening?"

Chickadee nodded. She pointed in the direction of the House-taurant. "Mavis is cooking the hot meals. Not sure what she is making tonight."

"Beef stew." Brandon reached into a nearby cooler. He dropped two beef roasts on the table.

"Why beef stew?" Atim asked as he pulled his legs out from under the picnic table.

"Well, our Head Chief at the time had never eaten

beef—only buffalo, moose—you know, wild meat. But he had seen a cow once on a trip to Red River, and he always wondered what cows tasted like." Brandon picked up the two roasts and turned to head out to the road. "He had said so to one of the Canadian traders. Word got back to Canada's treaty commissioner. So, as a show of friendship, the treaty commissioner brought a cow to butcher and eat at the treaty negotiations. Now, as a way of remembering that part of the Treaty 12 history, we always serve beef stew during the welcoming ceremony. Then the next day we start opening the bundle, because the treaty commissioner back in the old days was big on digestion and wouldn't talk business until the next morning."

The Muskrats followed their new friend out of the Shining Deer camp, and then Atim took the lead, pointing out the correct way to the House-taurant.

Chickadee held out her hands as an offer to carry one of the roasts. Brandon passed half the meat to her. The group chatted happily about their home communities as they made their way to the eatery.

Leaving the guest camp, Chickadee spotted Pearl and her crew hustling out of the campgrounds through the far corner of the field. A double-handled cooler was stretched between Bug and one of the other minions.

Chickadee pointed with her lips. "Hey. I wonder if that's theirs or somebody else's."

The other Muskrats looked. Sam groaned.

"Who's that?" Brandon shielded his eyes with his hands to get a better look.

"Just some…hoodlums." Atim shook his head, disappointed.

"Are they stealing that?" Brandon face darkened.

"Probably," Sam said, his brow twisted. "Ever embarrassing!" He threw up his hands.

"We don't know that…for sure." Otter shrugged, doubting his own words, but he felt he had to say them.

Atim and Samuel snorted. "Yeah, right."

Chickadee held out her hand. "We'll mention it to Uncle Levi." Her tone warned her cousins the subject was finished. She looked at Brandon. "Our Uncle Levi is the local band constable."

"Hope so! Our camp is in there!" Brandon's face filled with concern.

"We'll tell our Uncle about them," Otter assured him. "He'll deal with them."

It was a short walk to the homemade coffee shop. The door to the House-taurant opened with the tinkle of a bell on a spring. The small diner had been created when Mavis and her daughters moved into their basement, set up tables and chairs on the first floor, and started to serve food to customers.

The owner was a large, brown lady who jiggled all over when she walked. Her smile was welcoming but rested below eyes that quickly weighed a customer's character.

"Muskrats in my restaurant!" Mavis smirked as she yelled over her shoulder at the kitchen, her voice dripping with faux disgust.

"Oh no!" An unseen daughter went along with the gag from around the corner. The House-taurant was a hub of gossip in Windy Lake. If there was a scandal or a family tragedy, word of it was sure to float past the dangly earrings of Mavis and her sizable girls.

"Ha, ha! Ever funny." Atim exaggerated his fake laughter and slapped his knee.

"Good one." Otter smiled at the middle-aged lady as he took a seat at a table. Chickadee and Brandon joined him.

"Girl's gotta try, right?" The House-taurant's owner dropped some menus on the table.

Samuel smirked beside her. "Try harder."

Mavis was as old as their parents, but the Muskrats had been teased by her for so long, they weren't afraid to tease back.

"Sorry, Mavis, we ain't staying." Chickadee gathered up the menus and handed them back. "This is our friend, Brandon. He's Elder Shining Deer's apprentice and they're welcoming a treaty bundle tonight."

"A treaty bundle, hey?" Mavis, impressed, raised her eyebrows and let out a low whistle. She arched a brow at Brandon. "My daughters would *like* you."

The handsome, young man turned red. His mouth opened, but nothing came out.

"I brought some meat," Brandon finally managed to blurt.

"And you know your way to an old woman's heart." Mavis smiled down at him.

"You're not old, Mavis." Atim, still standing, rubbed her shoulder.

"Listen to this charmer." Mavis threw a thumb in Atim's direction. "Now, why are you bringing me meat?"

"We need stew to serve at the bundle welcoming ceremony. It has to be beef." Brandon had regained his composure.

"WHAT?!" She poked her finger in Atim's chest. "I bet this is your grandfather's meddling," Mavis exploded. "It's late in the afternoon! They're already cutting up the moose meat. We needed a whole other kitchen and stove. Do you know what it takes to feed that many people?!"

"Grandpa was the one that sent us," Atim stammered.

"Well, if he said it, it might as well have come from the organization committee." Mavis shook her head with actual disgust.

"Sorry, Mavis." Chickadee reached out and touched her arm.

"It was a quick decision." Sam was sympathetic.

Mavis held up the two roasts and look at Brandon. "This isn't enough to feed everyone!"

"Sorry." Brandon spoke with more than a little apprehension. "My grandfather has to provide some. He's the

Bundle Holder but he would go broke if he tried to feed everyone everywhere we went."

Mavis glowered at him and then looked down at the roasts.

The Muskrats and Brandon held their breath, not wanting to interrupt her thinking, or draw her wrath. But, when she finally spoke, her voice was thoughtful with only a touch of annoyance.

"We were going to have beef stew later in the week, so we got the stuff. I can send these over there, quick. Tell my sister we have a change of plans. She can throw the frozen moose meat back in the freezer. We just have to rearrange our meal plan." She was talking to herself more than the Muskrats.

Mavis nodded and looked up at Atim. "Okay. Beef stew and bannock. Tell your Grandpa he's a stinker. But we can do this."

The Muskrats began to breathe again.

"I apologize for throwing a wrench into your plans." Brandon held his palms skyward.

"Just let me know if there is anything valuable in that bundle that might turn a profit." Mavis's mouth laughed, but her eyes didn't. "With the extra workers and shipping more food up here, I'm just going to break even on this silly Assembly. And I thought I would make a big killing!"

After that, Brandon and the Muskrats left with quick, slightly uncomfortable good-byes.

Mavis had other things to think about, and just waved over her shoulder as she made her way around the corner to her kitchen.

"Sorry about that!" Otter said, incredulous.

"She was only joking!" Atim threw up his arms.

"Yeah, but still, joking about selling a treaty bundle." Chickadee shook her head.

"Ahh." Brandon waved his hand and chuckled. "She seemed like a nice lady."

Sam pinched his chin the way he always did when he thought seriously about something. "You know, I don't think Mavis would steal anything. She is too hard a worker. But she is a gossip, and it would stink if she said something that put bad ideas into someone else's head."

"Sheesh. Let's hope Pearl and her crew don't stop for burgers." Atim smacked his forehead.

Sam looked as his brother. He couldn't help but think that Pearl and her bunch were bad, but they were still the kiddie team. There were a lot worse.

CHAPTER 5

The Three Stew-ges

"It can be nice to be inside." Elder Leon was in his buckskin and beaded regalia as he stood in the center of the big teepee and spoke to the crowd.

The tent from Butterfly Narrows was packed with people. A gaggle of Elders sat in a dozen or so folding chairs, almost everyone younger sat on the grass, a few men stood along the canvas curve at the back. The sunlight filtering through the walls gave everything an orange glow.

Elder Leon's long, silver hair now hung in braids over his chest. "In the cold of winter, the teepee keeps us warm, keeps us alive. There is a lot of power in the door there." He gestured toward the large oval they had all entered through, now covered with a canvas flap.

Otter had the honor of being his grandfather's tobacco carrier and pipe filler. He looked along the row of Pipe Carriers that sat with his grandfather. At the far end sat the frog-like Elder from Butterfly Narrows. He looked like a grouchy stoic, sitting in a lump, seemingly oblivious to Elder Leon's words.

After a thoughtful pause, Elder Leon continued, scanning the room. "If we close the door too soon, we keep people on the outside, people we love that need to be warm. On the other hand, if we do not let those who are on the inside get out, they might feel uncomfortable and want to leave. Or maybe we let too many people come in, there will not be enough food for everyone to eat. So, there is a lot of power in knowing when to open the doorway, and when to keep it closed."

Otter listened from his kneeling position behind his grandfather. He was happy to just sit and watch. Normally, he'd be tending the fire and doing the other chores associated with unfolding a ceremony, but this gathering was so large there were other people doing those tasks.

When Otter leaned to the side and looked around his grandfather, he could see Chickadee with the women drummers from Windy Lake. They all sat on the grass in a row across the teepee, legs bent underneath them, their drums resting on their colorful ribbon skirts. Otter noticed that Mrs. Shining Deer, Aunt Dee, had joined the local women and now sat beside his cousin.

The other boys waiting behind their Pipe Carriers were all dressed in their finest ribbon shirts. Otter knew every color had a meaning to the wearers and their families. He nodded to the slightly older boy beside him, and then continued to look around.

The people were crowded together in the tight space of the teepee. Chickadee had told Otter about the people outside trying so hard to listen to the ceremony the evening before. He wondered if the people were out there now, struggling to hear the Elder's words.

"I want to thank the people of Butterfly Narrows for providing this wonderful teepee. I want to thank their Pipe Carriers, Medicine People, and Knowledge Holders for all they have done to maintain our ceremonies through the dark times, when they were outlawed by the Government of Canada." Elder Leon met the eyes of the each of the Pipe Carriers and nodded to each of them, including the one that seemed to sit in a cloud of anger. They all nodded back. He went on to thank a bunch of people, including Grandpa and the other host Elders.

Elder Leon's handsome smile had everyone smiling back. He slowly turned, speaking to everyone in the tent. "You know, my grandmother was one who always had a pot of stew on the fire. She always had food for visitors. It was our way to feed anyone who came to our door and asked for food." His eyes met those of the head Elder of Butterfly Narrows, who eventually nodded in agreement.

"I have seen the bundle bring people together," Elder Leon continued. "And, you know, I have certainly seen the stories and history that people share become spiritual and emotional food for people inspired by the presence of the bundle. It is a way for them to connect to the part of them that is a piece of something bigger. The stories fill them with pride and connect them to the people of the past. Of course, some need this kind of healing more than others."

Elder Leon stopped and looked thoughtfully around at the crowd. He lifted a finger skyward. "Today, while we appreciate the comfort of being inside, there are many people outside who want to share in the inspiration of the bundle." With that the Elder threw up his arms and gave a loud *hiy-hiy*!

Suddenly, the walls of the teepee were being rolled up. Quick hands on the outside gathered the canvas. Those inside were surprised to see the multitude outside.

Otter noticed that, since they had arrived, chairs had been brought for the Elders who didn't make it into the tent. They now surrounded the teepee with a look of expectation. A larger crowd stood behind them. Within a few seconds, the small circle of those crowded in the tent had become a legion of Cree people waiting to be enriched through the ceremony and the stories of the bundle.

"Look at those happy Cree faces," Elder Leon threw up his hands and laughed. Most of the people in the now-united crowd nodded and smiled in appreciation.

A lump of pride rose in Otter's throat. He couldn't help but notice that Atim, Simon, and their new friend,

Brandon, were among those rolling up the teepee walls. Obviously, it was something that they had planned with Elder Leon.

Otter looked over at the Elders from Butterfly Narrows, who were nodding and smiling. However, when he looked at their Pipe Carrier, his face was unreadable. Otter was sure he had turned a deeper shade of red.

"The truth is too big for just one man to hold." Elder Shining Deer moved on to the subject that was the focus of the evening's gathering. "Our people have always known that one person's truth is not the entire truth." His dark, piercing eyes scanned the crowd. "Each Treaty has its own histories, its own stories. The history of my lands is not the history of, say, our host's lands—the Windy Lake and its shores. It has different lessons."

Elder Leon moved his left hand along his right forearm as though he was creating different sections. "Tonight, we will welcome the bundle with a ceremonial feast. Tomorrow, we will open it up and I will begin the first day of telling the stories that go along with the bundle. It is a history I can only tell in our language, the language of our mothers and their grandmothers before them." The Elder seemed to reach back in time with a gesture of his arm.

Otter looked around for the other Muskrats. The boys were nowhere to be seen.

A bright camera flash went off and was noticed by everyone in the tent.

Elder Leon chuckled and held up his hand to shade his eyes. "That's my wife. She has my phone. She's very proud of me."

The crowd laughed gently.

With a small lean, Otter could see Chickadee and Aunt Dee. After taking another photo, the older woman leaned over and said something in Chickadee's ear. They both looked at the photo and giggled. Otter wondered what Aunt Dee had said. Raising the phone to take another picture, Aunt Dee suddenly stopped and studied the screen as a confused look spread across her face. She began to angrily swipe at the touchscreen with her finger. Otter hid a smile as he thought of his own grandfather's struggle with technology.

★

"What's the best way to do this?" Samuel stared at the pile of bowls, cutlery, ladles, and a huge cauldron of stew. "We have to feed the Elders and Pipe Carriers first...and they're in the center of all that." He waved, indicating the breadth of the crowd.

"They're pretty squished in there too." Atim stood with his hands on his hips looking over the multitude.

"And there's only the two of us...." Sam wished he had a troop of waiters to help. Mavis had dropped off the food and bowls, and then yelled that she had forgotten the bannock and needed to go back to the House-taurant.

And then Brandon ran off, after he yelled that he had a mission, so that left Samuel and Atim to figure out how to serve the food to the masses.

"I figure one of us carries the stew, aaannd…." Atim leaned over, ripped open the top flaps and tore off a side of the bowl box, so it made a quick shelf. Then he stuck the smaller box of bamboo sporks along one side. "The other one carries the box of bowls and cutlery."

Samuel raised his eyebrows, impressed. "Good thinking."

His older brother smiled. "Second idea!" Atim raised his finger into the air. "I'll carry the box, because we'll have to lift that over people's heads."

Samuel looked at the cauldron. It was a lot heavier than the box. His brother not only had the height, he seemed to get all the muscles too. Sam considered the task. "I suppose, I'll be able to find places to put it down if I have to."

"Sure you will." Atim slapped his brother on the shoulder.

Sam kept his eyes on the crowd, thinking. He reached out and gave his brother a shove. "Otter's in there."

"Chickadee too."

"Yeah, but Otter's right in there…in the ceremony, I mean."

"Yeah, he knows that stuff."

"He grew up with it." Sam's voice carried a touch of disappointment.

"Jelly?" Atim gave him another slap on the shoulder.

"No, not jealous. Regretful, maybe. I would have learned, if I was there, you know." Sam looked at his brother, seriously.

"I know. Me too."

Sam went over to try the weight of the big, black cauldron of stew. Its cast iron handle creaked as he picked it up. Its height was too long, he couldn't let its weight hang off his bony frame. He had to stretch out his back and bend his elbows to get the bottom of the huge pot just four inches off the ground. A quiver of doubt swept through him.

"Can you do it?" Atim asked.

The question rankled. Samuel took a deep breath and tried to look unconcerned with the weight. "No problem. Don't worry about it." He put it down for a second, switched hands, then lifted the load. Awkwardly, he began to limp toward the teepee.

As he and Atim got closer, they began to hear Elder Leon telling the story of the old Chief, the treaty commissioner, and the cow.

The chairs outside the tent had been arranged in sections with rows that Atim and Sam easily walked down. When they got under the rolled-up teepee walls, they had to stop to let their eyes adjust the shade.

Sam was dismayed to see the neat rows disappear

inside the tent. The only path led from where the door had been to the center of the ceremony.

Brandon was already inside. He spotted them and came over.

Sam breathed a sigh and set the stew down on a small patch of path. His relief quickly faded as Brandon lip-pointed in the direction of the Elders.

The Bundle Holder's apprentice whispered, "Feed the old people first, then the Pipe Carriers, women drummers, and then everyone else." He walked off, obviously, still on a mission.

"Let's go," Atim said to Samuel quietly.

Sam picked up his load.

Elder Leon was keeping the crowd enthralled; painting the past with interesting stories about the people at the treaty-making and the feelings of different factions from so long ago.

"But this is not an official telling, I'm just explaining why these young men are bringing stew around to you all. We'll eat this ceremonial stew. You may not get full, because there is only so much to go around. After that, we will begin the welcoming ceremony with these fine gentlemen here." Elder Leon indicated the Pipe Carriers, who nodded in acknowledgment.

Chickadee tiptoed through the crowd to help her cousins. Sam was happy when she took the ladle that had been clanking along the side of the cast-iron cauldron.

"Thank you," he whispered to his cousin.

Chickadee giggled. "Do you think I'd trust the hard work to just you boys?" She smiled. "Did you see Otter?" She lip-pointed in Grandpa's direction.

They all turned. Otter was leaning to one side so he could watch them. He waved when they turned to look. His cousins just nodded and beamed. They had work to do and full hands.

Once they got to the space where the fire would have been, Sam and Atim went clockwise to get to the Elders.

Atim presented his portable shelf of bowls to the first old woman in the front row. She took an empty bowl and put it in her lap. Following tightly behind Atim, Chickadee took the lid off Sam's cauldron and filled the ladle with stew. From her chair, the elderly woman held out her bowl. With a smile and a smattering of small talk, Chickadee filled it.

When the Muskrats went to move on, the Elder's brow furrowed. "No bannock?"

Chickadee raised her eyebrow and looked at Sam.

Sam's eyes grew large. "Don't look at me! Mavis had to run back to the House-taurant for the bannock. She said she forgot it."

Chickadee shook her head. "Ever not cool." Her face became the picture of disappointment as she turned to the lady. "No, I'm sorry, Elder. They forgot it back at the kitchen."

"So, you're giving me stew with no bannock?" The old lady's eyebrow arched like she was a Vulcan haggling over a bowl of soup.

Chickadee nodded, a large frown on her cheeks.

The Elder tapped Chickadee's hand. "It's okay. Don't worry about it. Bring me some bannock when it gets here."

Chickadee smiled at her, said good-bye, and moved on.

With one old woman satisfied, they all took a few steps around the circle to the woman's husband.

This is going to take a while, Samuel thought, his arms beginning to complain about their load. Changing strategy, he put the cauldron down and ferried bowls between Elders and Chickadee. Once two rows of Elders were fed, the Muskrats gathered for a quick conversation.

"This is taking so long!" Atim threw his hands in the air.

Sam rattled the ladle in the cauldron. "We're barely going to get through the Pipe Carriers with what's left!!"

"Where's the rest?" Chickadee's large eyes were filled with alarm.

Atim studied the crowd and spoke almost absentmindedly. "Mavis went to get the bannock; she must be bringing more stew too."

"Ho-leh. I hope so, or they're going to eat us!!" Chickadee looked around at all the people waiting for food.

The three of them laughed.

"Muskrat stew is good," Atim snickered.

"Cannibal." Sam punched his brother's arm. He looked over at Grandpa. Their Elder was staring back at them, expectantly. "Uh…we better get moving, Grandpa is giving me the look."

The Muskrats crossed to the other side of the teepee to feed the Pipe Carriers.

The stone and wood pipes sat in front of their owners in carved wood cradles that held them upright. The long pipe stems pointed out in a fan, but the different colored soapstone heads were clustered fairly close together, within easy reach, for their owners or their assistants to fill them.

Sam was realizing he should have been at the back of the stew parade, but instead, he was leading. He wanted to go behind the old men, but the first two were waving vigorously for him to hurry over.

The path between the Pipe Carriers and their pipes was a thin thread. Sam gulped.

The first two waved their hands insisting he come along. Unable to put down his load in the tight space, Sam walked forward slowly, holding the cauldron to one side. Chickadee would still be able to ladle out stew.

"Where's the bannock?"

The Muskrats groaned.

With the first two old men fed, Samuel continued to edge forward, unable to see his feet or his right side. He wanted to slip past Grandpa and the man beside him. But when Chickadee got to their grandfather, she pulled on Sam's sleeve for him to stop.

His cousin's tug pulled Samuel off balance. In slow-motion, he took one step toward the weight of the cauldron. He winced as he heard a series of clinks like dominoes falling over. A prickly heat spread across his face.

Sam looked over at the Pipe Carriers. The old man closest to him was tall and didn't have to look up much to meet Sam's eye even from his sitting position on the grass. His eyes burned red. All the Pipe Carriers glared at him, including his grandfather.

With more of the precious little strength left in his arms, Sam moved the cauldron over so he could look down. The fan of the pipe stems was akimbo, and the thin space that had once separated each stone pipe head had been collapsed by the push of his shoe.

Sam's mouth hung open in shock. He stammered an apology and moved forward quickly, he told himself, so the Carriers could straighten out their pipes without him in the way.

Finding a spot where he could stand and not hit any-thing sacred, he held the cauldron so his cousins could easily fill more bowls. Sam rubbed his forehead in conster-nation; he couldn't believe he had hit the pipes with his foot! If only Chickadee hadn't pulled his sleeve.

After all the V.I.P.s were fed, the sleuths moved to the other rows. But it didn't take long for Sam's prediction to come true.

"We're out." Atim dropped the ladle into the big pot.

A hungry crowd, waiting for their share of ceremonial cow, glared expectantly at the Muskrats.

CHAPTER 6

Lessons in Leadership

"I kicked the pipes!" Sam threw his arms in the air, exasperated.

Atim's jaw dropped. "How could you?"

"Chickadee tugged on my shirt as I was taking a step, and I lost my balance." Disappointment dripped from Sam's voice. "At least I didn't fall down. BUT I KICKED THE PIPES!"

The three cousins had hurried out of the teepee with the empty cauldron, the ladle rattling inside. They felt the eyes of the crowd as they scurried away to look for Mavis and more stew. Now, they were back at the drop-off spot and she was nowhere to be found.

"I didn't mean it!" Chickadee slapped her knees. Her face twisted with worry.

Sam walked over and gave her a hug that he needed just as much as she did.

Chickadee half pulled away from her cousin. "Sorry, Sam. I didn't mean it."

"I know you didn't. It was an accident." He smiled at her. "But you know how the Elders always say that little things carry messages. How serious is this?"

Atim was grave. "What does it mean when someone kicks some of the most sacred items in the ceremony?"

Sam's shoulders fell. "I don't know."

As the cousins were contemplating the gravity of Sam's sin, Brandon came walking up. "What's going on? Where's the beef?"

"Mavis hasn't brought the rest of the food." Chickadee shook her head.

"It's a disaster!" Atim cried.

Brandon chuckled. "You guys are getting a taste of leadership."

"Huh?!" Atim's face twisted.

The young man smiled at the Muskrats. "Imagine in the old days, there were no paid police, there were no standing armies, like city people had. Cree leaders had to show their followers that they could keep them fed, that they could keep the children's tummies full, and keep them all alive."

Sam thought back to the people who had been next in line for stew, empty bowls sat in their laps, their eyes expectant, hungry. And behind him, the people with stew were bannock-less. They might just have been the waiters, but there were some in the crowd who looked at the Muskrats with derision and reproach.

"Leaders must have been under a lot of pressure," Sam said. He remembered how his concern had risen as each scoop of stew was ladled out. The huge pot seemed to get smaller and smaller, but the number of mouths to feed just seemed to grow.

Brandon looked back at the tent. "It took a lot of knowledge, a lot of teamwork, and a lot of hard-working hands set to the task of survival. Leaders back in the day had to inspire people to come together. They had to convince people that they knew how to provide a good life, or the people wouldn't follow."

Sam squinted as he looked at Brandon in the sunlight. "Having hundreds of people that you care about—your family and community—knowing that you have to pull all your food and shelter out of the forest. That's huge!"

"And clothes and good water and safe places to raise your kids." Chickadee ticked them off on her fingers, adding to the responsibilities of past leaders.

Their conversation was interrupted by the wheeze of Mavis' truck. Reinforcements had arrived with stew and bannock. The Muskrats heaved sighs of relief.

A few minutes later, the beef stew was being handed out to the crowd. Not wanting to run out of food again, Chickadee's ladle was a little stingier than it had been earlier. Sam was happy his older brother had taken the cauldron this time. He handed out bowls and the thin, bamboo, disposable forks.

By the time everyone had a bowl of stew and a piece of bannock, Elder Leon had stood up and was once again speaking to the crowd. "As soon as everyone is done eating, we'll have the important ceremony welcoming the bundle to the territory. You've all been sitting for a long time now, and it's going to take about ten minutes to get everything ready, so when you've finished the stew, go stretch your legs for a bit." With his long arms, his gestures shooed out the entire crowd.

Most of the families took him up on his offer. Many of the Elders stayed put.

Otter came and joined his cousin.

"How was that?" Sam studied his cousin.

"I got pins and needles in my legs," Otter groaned and punched his own thighs.

"Really? Where does it hurt?" Atim playful grabbed his cousin's legs, causing Otter to cry out in pain and giggle at the same time.

The Muskrats filtered out with the crowd.

Once they were out of the throng and into the open, Chickadee pointed. "Hey, look! There's Brandon. Maybe he needs help." Chickadee raced the other Muskrats to the Shining Deers' truck.

Brandon had a door open and was shifting things around as he looked for something. He saw the children run up and yelled over his shoulder. "I need a certain color of green."

"Anything we can do to help?" Chickadee spoke loudly to reach his ear.

"Get some of those bolts of cloth in the back. We'll take them to my grandfather." Brandon waved toward the rear of the vehicle.

Atim, Chickadee, Otter, and Sam found a large, blue, plastic box with its lid pushed back. It was filled with many folded lengths of cloth. Atim and Chickadee grabbed four each. Sam looked in and grabbed the next four; a dark blue, a light green, a black, and a white.

Brandon looked at what the Muskrats had brought. When he came to Sam, he shook his head.

"Not this one. You never give black to a Cree Elder. It represents death." Brandon threw the black cloth back into the box.

"I'm sorry. I didn't know." Sam's shoulders drooped.

"All good." Brandon patted him on the back. "Not everyone knows protocol. It goes like this; the sun is the source of energy that livens up the day, so, the dark of night can represent cold and hunger and death. Get it?"

"I didn't really grow up with it, you know?" Sam voice sounded slightly guilty.

"What? Ceremony?" Brandon's brow furrowed.

Atim and Sam nodded.

"They grew up in the city. So, it's not their fault," Chickadee defended her cousins.

"Of course, it isn't." Brandon shook his head. "Many communities are just getting their traditions back now. And many families, even those strong in ceremony, are still trying to figure out how to, you know, carry out their land-based spirituality in the city, where Creation's lessons are covered with concrete."

"We really want to learn," said Atim sincerely, brushing his hair aside.

"Yeah. We *need* to." Sam nodded.

Brandon smiled sympathetically at the boys. "That's good. All I can say is…just keep doing what you're doing. Help out when you can, start at the beginning, be quiet and listen when knowledge is being spilled."

"I kicked the pipes!" Sam blurted it out, and then was suddenly embarrassed.

"What?" Brandon shook his head like he was trying to shake off an annoying mosquito. "You did…what?!"

Atim snickered, and then covered his mouth with his hand, trying to stifle further snickering.

Sam sighed. "I kicked the sacred pipes…in the teepee, when I was carrying the big cauldron around."

"It was my fault," Chickadee said, her eyes serious. "I pulled him off balance."

"It just happened…." Sam gave his cousin a tight smile.

Brandon burst out laughing.

The Muskrats were shocked for a moment, and then they too, erupted in giggles.

"I...can imagine...how that went over." The young man squeezed it out between guffaws.

"Even Grandpa looked like he wanted to kill me." Sam smiled, chagrined.

Brandon's chuckles sputtered to a stop. "Don't worry about it. By the time the ceremony is done, they'll have forgotten."

"I don't know...." Sam didn't sound convinced. "What does it mean, if someone kicks the pipes?"

"What does it mean?"

"Well...you know, like, if a baby is kicking in the mummy's tummy, it means the ancestors' spirits are fighting over who will be reborn in that baby. Well, what does it mean if someone kicks the pipes in a ceremony?"

Brandon's handsome features twisted as he thought about the question. "I suppose the superstitious or the fundamentalist might say the ceremony is damaged and won't do what it was intended to do...."

"Aww, man!" Sam slapped his forehead.

"...But most Elders would just say it was an accident. You were carrying the big pot?"

Sam nodded.

"So, you were really working *for* the ceremony when it happened. What did you do when you did it?"

"I don't know. I felt sick. I said something like 'Sorry!' But I didn't even really listen to myself."

Brandon chuckled. "It's not like you were a stranger that came in and kicked the pipes for the heck of it. It was packed in there. You were doing work." He patted Sam on the shoulder.

Chickadee gave her cousin a half-hug.

Samuel started feeling a little better. "I thought I was going to freak out right there," he admitted.

"Did you look really sorry when you did it?" Brandon raised an eyebrow.

"Oh, yeah. My face fell. I turned bright red. My jaw dropped."

"Well, then. They're Elders. If they saw that, they'll take that into consideration."

"When they finish being angry?"

"Yes, when they finish being angry. And they'll tease you about it for the rest of your life." Brandon laughed.

Atim and Chickadee each gave Sam a little shove.

"Don't worry about it, Samuel." Chickadee smiled at him.

Atim snickered. "Think of all the dumb stuff our older cousins have done. Grandpa hasn't killed any of them."

"All right, I'm good. Nothing to do but wait to see how Grandpa reacts when I see him." Sam smiled. "Sooo... what's all this cloth for?"

Atim punched the palm of his hand. "He's back!!" Everyone laughed.

Brandon explained that tomorrow the bundle would be opened, people would get a chance to see what was inside, and then, over the next few days, Elder Leon would tell all those who would sit and listen the oral history that went with the bundle.

"As they start to tell the stories, the bundle will be rewrapped with these new cloths." Brandon pointed to the folded fabric. "As each little item's story is told, it will be rewrapped back into the bundle, back into the history packet. After that, there will be a day of different ceremonies that go with the protocols of completely closing the bundle and saying good-bye to the territory."

Brandon began to take the cloths from the Muskrats and pile them along his arms. "I have to take these into the tent. Tonight, the ceremony will go long. But when it's opened tomorrow, the bundle will definitely bring the people together."

Otter listened to Brandon intently, looking forward to watching the rest of the ceremony. But the face of the lead Elder from Butterfly Narrows plodded through Otter's mind. He hoped Elder Leon's apprentice was right, and unity would be found at the National Assembly of Cree Peoples.

The sky was just beginning to darken.

CHAPTER 7
Bundle Burgled

"The bundle! The bundle has been stolen!!"

The crazy creak of Grandpa's door woke Otter like a gunshot. He launched straight out of bed. It took a few seconds for the words to sink in. And then a few more to realize it wasn't Grandpa who had said them.

"Who is that? Leon?" Grandpa's voice could be heard through the bedroom door. Otter quickly put on some clothes and stepped out into the hallway. On the other side of the kitchen, in the front doorway, Elder Leon held tightly to Grandpa's shoulders.

"The bundle! It's gone!!" The distraught man gave Otter's grandfather a slight shake.

Grandpa, still in his PJs, stepped back, blinking and trying to shake off sleep. "Come in, Leon." He motioned for his friend to follow, turned to the kitchen table and indicated a seat. "Start at the beginning, my friend. Let's talk about this."

Elder Leon sat down, desperately hoping Grandpa could help.

Grandpa waved at his grandson. "Make some tea, my boy."

Otter walked to the kitchen counter. He had made tea for his grandfather so many times he could do it with his eyes closed. But he missed his late grandmother every time he did it. He imagined Grandma now, taking a seat beside the men, ready to deal out her own brand of wisdom.

"Now tell me, Leon. What happened?" Grandpa asked.

The confidence and charisma had been pulled from the Bundler Holder's face. Desperation had bled the good looks from his features.

Elder Leon held his head in his hands. "I was getting ready for the sunrise ceremony. I went to the Butterfly Narrows teepee where we let the bundle rest before today's ceremony. When I walked in, I went to where I left it…. It was gone!"

Grandpa reached across the table and grasped one of his friend's arms in sympathy. "Where were the guards?"

"They were there! That boy Casey from Butterfly Narrows and his friends insisted on watching the teepee. It's usually Brandon who finds someone. But the boys from Butterfly Narrows insisted. So, I thought why not? Peaceful gesture, right? Maybe not!"

"Now, now, Leon. We have to be careful not to lay blame before we know. We don't know that they took it."

Otter suddenly remembered Pearl and her crew disappearing across the field with the cooler. The Muskrats hadn't told their Uncle Levi about the theft yet. He placed a cup of tea in front each of the men.

"Someone took it! We have to figure out who—and quick."

"I just got a new phone. My son, Levi, is the band constable here. We can give him a call. If we need, he can get the RCMP involved."

Otter went to the recently installed phone on the wall, handed the receiver to his grandfather, and began to dial the number. After that call, Otter called Atim and Samuel. He told them to pick up Chickadee and meet him at the crime scene. The Mighty Muskrats were on the case.

★

The sun was just poking over the horizon when they all arrived at the arbor grounds. The fall air was crisp. The site of the National Assembly of Cree Peoples seemed swathed in cloud. A mist had floated off the lake and now filtered in between the big teepee and the silent circle of the arbor. Rolling amidst forest and homes, the fog muffled the colors and sounds of a community that was just waking up.

With some effort, Uncle Levi lowered his frame so he could examine the tracks on the ground. "We need to keep everyone from walking around here. We don't want people destroying sign." He lifted his hat and scratched his head. His salted, crew-cut hair still showed the signs of having recently been pressed against a pillow.

The boys from Butterfly Narrows had been waiting in a cluster. Brandon stood close by and sighed with relief when he saw his grandfather return with help.

Knowing they could be sent home, the Muskrats did their best to stay out of the way and watch the hubbub from its edge.

"What have you done with the bundle?!" Elder Leon couldn't hold back his anger any longer. He pointed an accusing finger at the young men tasked with guarding the teepee. The Muskrats' eyes were wide with surprise at the outburst. Brandon stepped behind his grandfather.

"What are you talking about?" Casey spoke for the group, but the others uttered angry defenses under their breath. "We didn't do anything!"

Uncle Levi stood with a slight groan and placed the hat back on his head. He hitched up his belt and walked over to the confrontation.

Grandpa tried to calm his angry friend. "Now, Leon...we don't know anything about anything yet."

The Muskrats' grandfather placed a hand on Elder Leon's shoulder.

The old man turned toward his friend but flung out an angry arm at the guys from Butterfly Narrows. "If they didn't take it, they should know who did, right? They were supposed to be guarding it."

Grandpa had no answer to that.

Atim nodded in agreement. Chickadee scowled.

Uncle Levi moseyed up and stood between Elder Leon and the young men from Butterfly Narrows. "This is now a crime scene, so I'm in charge." He looked at the former Bundle Holder. "The best way you can help me is to calm down. Let me take some time to look around…talk to people."

Elder Leon was still angry but after a moment, he nodded.

The band constable nodded back. Then he turned and walked over to Casey. "I'll need to ask you boys a few questions. Okay?"

Casey spread his hands in surrender. "We'll help however you want, officer. We had nothing to do with this."

"Good. Wait here." Uncle Levi spun around and walked directly toward the Muskrats. The four youngsters tried to look like they just happened to be standing in the morning fog.

"You four going to be a problem?" Their uncle stood with his hands on his hips.

Atim stepped forward, confidently. "We could be a help, Uncle."

Otter's thin frame took a spot beside his cousin. "Heck of a lot of new people in Windy Lake."

In two strides, Chickadee was beside them both, her dark eyes serious. "That's a lot of suspects. Hey, Uncle Levi?"

"Even Sherlock Holmes had the Baker Street Irregulars." Samuel joined the other Muskrats.

Uncle Levi guffawed. "Irregulars, all right."

"It couldn't hurt to have an extra set of eyes and ears." Sam watched his uncle to see the effect of his words. "A smaller, less experienced, but very curious...."

"Nosey, more like." Their uncle pulled some lint from his band constable uniform.

"...Set of investigators," Sam continued, "but a useful tool, nonetheless."

"Nonetheless...." Their uncle took a step away, and then turned back. "I'm about to question these young men. I can't help it if they choose to speak with you nerds around."

The Muskrats let out a whispered cheer, but then quickly put away their jubilation and put on an air of professionalism.

Casey and his friends had gathered in a defensive circle at the edge of the parking lot. Occasionally, one of them threw a glance over his shoulder.

Uncle Levi's footsteps crunched in the gravel as he

marched over to the four young men. The failed guards were so keyed up they all almost stood on their tiptoes. Their shoulders were bunched around their ears.

It could be because it's cold, Sam thought, *but they're very tense.*

The band officer looked at each of them, quietly waiting. In the face of his silence, the boys' defiance had nothing to keep it going. After a moment of quiet, their demeanor softened.

That was when Uncle Levi chose to speak. "So…last night?" He let the words hang in the air.

The guards waited for the sentence to end. But Uncle Levi's pause was expectant. The young men's hearts pushed their minds to close the awkward circle.

Casey began a stammered response. "After everyone left, we were all alone. We stayed at the four corners of the tent, like the Elder said." Casey looked around at the others for confirmation. They all nodded vigorously, affirming his story.

Casey continued. "It was a long night. First thing this morning, the Bundle Carrier, Shining Deer, showed up, went into the tent, and when he came out, he said the bundle was gone. He didn't say much after that. Just hopped in his truck and drove away."

Casey looked up at Uncle Levi. "And now, here we are, getting accused of stealing something we were protecting all night." He threw up his hands in frustration. "Well…

most of the night. Trying to protect...." Casey shrugged.

"Welp!" Uncle Levi said it loudly and looked directly at Casey. Quietly, he continued. "I got good news and bad news. Good news, I *suspect*...you didn't steal the bundle." He hitched up his belt.

The young men sighed in relief and smiled amongst themselves.

"Bad news. I need all your shoes...just to make sure." Uncle Levi smiled.

"What?!" the young men exclaimed at once.

Uncle Levi collected four pairs of runners. Grumbling, the failed guards of Butterfly Narrows marched off to their camps in stocking feet.

"Why did you let them go, Uncle?" Sam's head was cocked to one side.

Uncle Levi smiled at Sam. "Why do you think?"

Sam thought for a moment.

Otter spoke up. "They didn't feel guilty to me."

Uncle Levi frowned and looked at his nephew. "What does that mean?"

Otter shrugged a shoulder. "I don't know. If they had stolen the bundle, I guess they would have acted differently. They didn't seem to make up a story...."

"Yeah, and nobody made excuses for stuff or seemed nervous when you made them hand over their shoes." Chickadee squinted up at her uncle as the fog-filtered morning sun pushed above the tree line.

"Just angry." Atim snickered. But he stopped when Uncle Levi gave him a sharp look.

"We'll check their shoes against the tracks we find around the teepee." Uncle Levi stared at the scene, but he was obviously already inside his head making plans and arranging details.

"What do you think you'll find?" Sam asked.

"Don't want to prejudge that, I suppose." Uncle Levi began to walk back to his vehicle. "But, if things don't seem to match what they told me, I can speak to those guys again when they come for their shoes. Sometimes it's best to break up buddies. When you get them all alone, you might find their stories don't follow the same path."

Sam raised his eyebrows, impressed with their uncle's tactics.

"Well…I know you Muskrats are going to go stick your noses in this." Uncle Levi met each of their eyes in turn. "Now! You better stay out of my crime scene. If I catch you ruining evidence—"

The Muskrats started to deny they would ever do such a thing.

Uncle Levi raised a finger. "Even by accident! I'll have to forget you're my family and focus on my duty to Windy Lake." He stared at them sternly. "Understand?"

The Muskrats nodded.

Uncle Levi broke into a smile. "If you find out anything interesting, I want to know it too." He waggled his head a bit. "And if there is any info I can tell you, I'll fill you in. Okay?"

The Muskrats smiled up at their uncle and agreed vigorously.

He shooed them away and turned back to the crime scene.

The cousins took a short walk away from their uncle and were about to discuss where they would go next, when Sam motioned toward their grandfather and Elder Shining Deer. The two old men were still engaged in heavy conversation.

"Why didn't he keep them here?" Elder Leon's words were flinted.

"Levi knows what he's doing." Grandpa looked up at his friend, serious, but kind. Leon turned from his friend in frustration, raised a hand to his forehead, and held his head.

Sam walked toward their Elders. The other Muskrats reluctantly followed in his wake.

"Elder Leon?" Samuel figured they needed to get what they could, while the man's memory was still fresh.

Elder Shining Deer looked over and raised an eyebrow. Sam cleared his throat nervously. "When did you see the bundle last?"

The old man's anger ebbed as he combed the details of his memory. "I…after the crowd left. It was dark. I like to say goodnight to the bundle. So, I shared a pipe with it and then I left the tent."

"Is that when you spoke to the boys from Butterfly Narrows about staying the night?" Atim stepped forward now that it seemed Elder Leon was willing to talk.

"No…that happened earlier. I spoke to them, but that was before I went to say goodnight." The older man nodded confidently. "So, it was all set up. I told them to stand at each corner of the teepee and keep a sharp eye out for man or spirit."

"And when you came back this morning?" Sam pinched his lower lip as he waited for further input.

"When I came back, they were all standing around the front door."

"All of them?" Chickadee asked from the back, her hands buried in the warm bunny pocket of her hoodie.

"All of them. Well…actually, there was one…." Elder Leo squinted as he thought. "The boy with the buckskin jacket, he was still around the back when I came."

"Who would want to steal the bundle?" Chickadee looked off into the distance as she searched her mind. "A bone-digger?"

Grandpa shook his head. He looked tired. The drama of the morning had sapped his energy. "I wouldn't think so. But someone might take it with the idea of selling it."

The Muskrats shared a glance. Chickadee looked at her feet, remembering Pearl and her crew running across the field with a cooler. When she looked up, Otter met her eyes and shook his head.

Stepping forward, Sam waved an arm at the other Muskrats and smiled up at the older men. "Well, I think we have to go for a walk and talk and see if we can find out more."

Elder Leon looked at Grandpa, impressed. "So, this is it? This is how they work?"

Grandpa rubbed the back of his neck. He smiled, proud, but a bit chagrined. "These are them, the Mighty Muskrats. They'll pull something out of the swamp. No doubt about that."

"It might be stinky," Otter ventured with fake seriousness.

Everyone laughed. The Muskrats said quick good-byes and assured their Elders they would come to them with any evidence gathered.

Chickadee looked at the boys. "To the fort? Talk this out?"

The other Muskrats nodded. They trotted off the grounds.

The sun was beginning to burn away the fog. When they had arrived, only the guards and a few others had been in the arbor grounds. Now, those who wanted to take part in the sunrise ceremony were starting to arrive.

The Muskrats knew it wouldn't take long before Windy Lake and the entire National Assembly of Cree Peoples were buzzing with the news of the missing bundle.

CHAPTER 8
Fort-itude

The Muskrats crouched in the long, dead grass surrounding the pile of discarded cars, trucks, heavy equipment, school buses, and other vehicles that had been, under the orders of the Department of Indigenous Affairs, pulled from around the reserve and dumped into a single location. The cracks and valleys of the junkyard were then filled, over time, with the refuse of the information age: drifts of old TVs, monitors, printers, computers, and electronic equipment. Thrown by a playful wind, a clatter of dead and hardened leaves danced across the rusting hulks, their sunbaked windshields, and the yellow of aging plastic.

Confident they were alone, the sleuths slunk across the expanse. On the edge of the pile of vehicles sat an ancient wood, tin, and steel Bombardier, its beetle shape covered in chipped, blue paint. Its hulking weight was slowly pushing its wide front skis and rear half-tracks into the soft earth. Atim held open the passenger-side door of the Bombardier and waved for the other investigators to hop inside. After a quick look around, he followed.

Inside the snow van, the Muskrats ignored the posters, pillows, benches, and magazines that turned the interior into a preteen's paradise. They studied the edge of the field out of round windows and a badly cracked windshield. Satisfied they were unseen, Otter opened the dirty, blackened screen that once separated the passenger quarters from the rear engine compartment. Instead of the rusting motor that once pushed the vehicle across the frozen north, an aluminum culvert led into the darkness of the junkyard. On their knees, the Muskrats crawled across a tunnel floor covered in boards and carpet into their fortress of solitude. Otter closed the filthy, oily screen to the tunnel behind them.

The far end of the culvert was stuck in the rear emergency doorway of a decommissioned school bus that was buried in the center of the junkyard. Almost all the bus seats had been removed and replaced with the battered couches and tables that now lounged along the walls. Stacks of crushed cars were all that could be seen through the dusty windows, with an occasional sliver of the field beyond.

Standing up after the crawl, Otter found the hand sanitizer that Chickadee had tied there. He squirted some onto his fingers where the oily screen had left grease stains and rubbed his hands together.

"We have to clean that thing," Chickadee said absent-mindedly, as she turned her attention to a time-beaten computer that had just started to rattle and hum.

"It's good camouflage." Atim grabbed a dumbbell from a sagging weight bench.

Although all the furniture within the bus was cobbled together from discarded bits from the junkyard outside, the Muskrats' fort was clean and functional. Sam had found his latest read and was now thumbing through its pages before curling up in the driver's seat.

"I don't know what I'm looking for!" Chickadee tossed the mouse at the keyboard and swiveled her chair around to look at her cousins. "What can you tell me, boys?"

"The info we need isn't in here." Otter tapped the yellowed monitor of Chickadee's computer, then spread his arms, taking in the wide world outside the fort. "It's out there. We have to go talk to the people of Windy Lake."

Atim stopped lifting weights, then blurted out, "Well, we better stop wasting time!"

"Why you so chippy?" Chickadee turned her attention to Atim.

"Sorry." Atim waved an apology at his cousin. "I'm just thinking, it could be Pearl and her cousins that stole the bundle…that would just make me so mad."

"We don't know if that was someone else's cooler we saw them carrying," Otter cautioned. "We have to treat people like they haven't done anything wrong, until we can prove they have."

"True. But we all know the stuff they've done. Remember when Pearl and her cousins flash mobbed the church's candy store?" Sam put aside his book.

"Or the raid on Ferland's garden?" Chickadee raised an eyebrow and crossed her arms.

Atim laugh. "That was just after Pearl and Bug got caught inside the school...in the middle of the night... on a weekend."

"But...when it comes to the bundle, they are still innocent until proven guilty. That's why I didn't mention the cooler to Uncle Levi. We really don't know."

Atim smacked his hands against his jeans and stood. "Well, they sure don't seem to care what other places think of Windy Lake!"

Chickadee shook her head. "Like Grandpa said, treaty is all about being a part of something larger, and some people...just aren't into that. They're looking out for number one." She held her index finger aloft.

Samuel put down his book. "I'd like to talk to those boys from Butterfly Narrows again."

"That means we have two threads to follow; the boys from Butterfly Narrows and Pearl and her gang."

Otter thought back to the grimace and anger expressed

by the frog-faced Elder from out West. "What about the Elder from Butterfly Narrows?"

"Well...I figured that's who the failed guards would be working for." Samuel waved his hand side to side. "Maybe they just looked the other way."

"But...what if the boys didn't know their Elder wanted to steal it? What if they didn't know anything about it? They'd be a cover for him no matter what...right?" Otter raised an eyebrow at his cousins.

Eventually, the other Muskrats nodded.

"That's right, Otter." Sam smiled. "Whether they knew about it or not, the failed guards would be a distraction for anyone looking for the missing bundle."

"Maybe the Elder isn't involved at all...." Chickadee shrugged.

"Or the guards," Sam added. "Casey seemed like a nice guy when I spoke to him."

"How are we going to figure this out?" Atim threw his hands in the air.

"Just...step by step. What does Grandpa say?" Sam looked at his brother. "If you're looking for something in the bush, look for difference, because after a while, everything looks the same. You need to keep an eye out for the tiny things that are shifted, or don't fit right."

"Well, the main difference is, where the bundle used to be, there ain't no bundle now!" Atim gestured toward the Assembly grounds. "Where do we look for difference next?"

"We need to find difference in the stories people tell us," Chickadee assured Atim.

Samuel was in agreement. "Yep. We could start by asking the guards why they were all bunched together...."

"But one of them wasn't!" Otter cautioned, with his eyebrows high.

"We know. That could be a difference in their story. So, if we ask them about it, it may point to other cracks." The recycled office chair creaked as Chickadee stood.

Sam slapped his books down as he rose. "We better go, this information is only valuable for a bit. Soon, everyone will know what happened. We have to get to Mavis at the House-taurant and spend our gossip while it's still new."

The other Muskrats laughed and got ready to leave.

★

The bell tinkled when the Muskrats opened the House-taurant door. The smell of cooking breakfasts rushed out of the warm home.

"Keep an eye out for the health inspector! We got Muskrats in da house!" Mavis shouted to her daughter in the kitchen when she spotted the sleuths.

The Muskrats groaned.

"That never gets old," Sam grumbled, shaking his head.

"Really?" Chickadee rolled her eyes within the depths of her favorite hoodie.

"Ever slack, Mavis!" Atim shouted, cheerfully.

Giggling and jiggling, Mavis's large form floated gracefully between the tables.

"You kids are here early. What's up? Or do you actually have enough money for a meal?"

Samuel picked the table closest to the door and slid onto a seat. "Sorry, Mavis. We're here for your traditional knowledge."

Chortling, the other Muskrats sat around him.

"Mmm-hmm. This one...," Mavis put a hand on her hip and waggled a finger at Samuel. "When this one starts to flatter me, I know he wants something." She looked around at the preteens staring up at her with painted smiles.

"We may have some news...." Sam shrugged and smirked playfully.

"Spill it. Let's quit the dancing." Mavis tightened her lips and looked at Sam out of the corner of her eye.

"How late were you here last night?"

"I sleep here," Mavis said in mock anger.

"I mean, when did you close last night?" Sam smiled up at her. He enjoyed sparring with the House-taurant owner.

"The usual, sometime around ten-ish. Had to let a

couple of tables finish eating, then clean up. I think we shut off the lights around eleven-thirty or so."

"Hmmm...." Sam looked at the ground, pinched his lip thoughtfully and then looked back up at her. "This morning...what time did you open?"

"Rabbit Man comes for coffee at five a.m., rain or shine. He wakes us up, if...uh...the *girls* sleep in." Mavis tapped her toe a couple of times and looked down at Sam. "All right, Muskrat, spill it. What do you got?"

Samuel smiled. To push Mavis further would be to invite her actual wrath. "Did anyone talk about stealing...," Sam paused, his finger in the air.

Mavis leaned forward in anticipation. Her great bulk loomed over the table. When she was almost on her tippy-toes, Samuel resumed.

"...The treaty bundle that was supposed to be opened at the Cree Assembly today?"

The Muskrats waited for the information to sink in to their sizable host.

"As if!? The treaty bundle...stolen. Holy! When did that happen?" Mavis blinked, then opened her eyes wide, she shook her head like she had just been punched.

"Last night." Chickadee leaned forward on the table.

Mavis pulled up a chair from the next table and plopped down. She let a big breath out through pursed lips. "Who would steal a treaty bundle?" She was still incredulous.

"That's what we need to find out." Atim leaned back in his chair. His stomach growled. Everyone at the table heard it.

Mavis acted like she received a great blow, blinking and leaning back, arms akimbo. The Muskrats broke out into laughter.

"You guys haven't eaten yet?" Mavis' voice held a touch of concern.

"Up too early." Atim shrugged. "I'm okay. Got no cash anyway."

"You got no money too? You? You?" Mavis pointed to each of the Muskrats. After they had all shook their heads, she put a hand to her mouth and yelled into the kitchen. "Daughter!? You throw away that burnt bacon yet?"

A slightly disinterested voice yelled back. "Not yet. It's sitting here with yesterday's leftover bannock."

"Bring it out for the Muskrats."

A slightly smaller version of Mavis lumbered out and dropped a plate of blackened, brittle pig strips and a quarter of dried-out, crumbly, baked bannock onto the table. Without a word, she teetered off back into the kitchen.

"Eat up!" Mavis smiled at the plate as though it was the proverbial loaves and fishes.

Atim reached for the bannock eagerly and ripped off a baseball-sized chunk.

The little bell hanging over the door tinkled. Mavis looked over her shoulder at her new arrivals. A group of old people from Windy Lake nodded and gave gentle hellos to all those watching them enter.

The restaurant owner put one great hand on her knee and, with the other, used the table to push herself to her feet. "I'll be back. Let me think about this. Going to get these people some coffee."

With loud hellos for her new guests, Mavis walked away. The Muskrats bent into the task of divvying up the bannock and bacon, and then sat back to eat and talk.

"Well, obviously, no one has said a thing, or she wouldn't have to think about it." Sam shook his head.

"Let her think a bit." Chickadee sopped up some of the bacon grease with a morsel of bannock. "She may remember something that could help."

"And we got bacon. Lovely, lovely bacon." The charcoal strip that Atim was chewing crunched loudly between his teeth.

The Muskrats continued to eat their donated meal.

Eventually, Mavis swung by on her rounds between her customers. "You kids ever heard of Guy?"

The Muskrats' brows furrowed. They shook their heads.

"What kind of name is Guy?" Sam asked.

"It's French. He pronounces it *Gee*, but it's spelled G-U-Y, so that's how I say it. Drives him nuts," Mavis said with a mischievous giggle. "Anyway, he's a little French fella. Says he's Métis. He's got a bit of Mohawk from out East, apparently. He's a loudmouth, always spouting off.

He comes in here around eight-thirty every morning for coffee."

"With the mine here, there are always guys from out of town spouting off about something." Atim waved a hand in the air in disgust.

"Yeah, but since the Assembly has been here, he's been going on about the Cree, and how the Mohawk drove them out of Ontario." Their host's eyes rolled. "Guy says he's got no respect for Neechies, anyway." Mavis shrugged.

"So, you think he might have taken the bundle?" Sam asked, thinking about the complications of a new suspect.

Mavis snorted. "He was in here the other morning saying how he was going to cause trouble at the Assembly. He's small, five-foot-nothing. But there's a lot of crazy in that little package. If anyone was going to do it, he would."

"Really?" Chickadee was still surprised that anyone would steal something so special. "But why?"

"He's the kind of guy who would bet his friends he could do it. He's an I'll-show-them kind of character. And nutty to boot. He'd do it to show up the Cree. He grew up in a big family of all brothers, he said. Probably always feels he's got to prove something to somebody."

"I guess we got to add him to the list." Otter scratched his head.

"Talk to him, at least." Atim looked concerned.

"He says he's Métis. But he's from out East." Samuel pointed a finger.

Mavis shrugged. "Lots of people with a little Indian blood in them say they're Métis now."

"That doesn't sound right." Otter's brow furrowed and he looked at the floor.

Mavis giggled a little. "Okay, I got customers." She wandered off with her coffee jug in hand.

"I think we've got all we can get here," Atim said, as he wiped the last of the bacon grease off the plate with the remaining corner of bannock.

"Yes, we now owe Mavis for a breakfast." Sam laughed at his brother.

Atim rolled his eyes. "It was only burnt bacon and bannock."

"It was a pretty nice thing to do anyway. We should do something nice," Chickadee admonished her bigger cousin.

Sam stared off into the distance as he spoke. "Yes, but when we have the time and something nice. Right now, we got to figure out more about this Guy guy. He's a new potential suspect."

Chickadee looked around at the rest of the group. "Well then, let's hit the road and head to the Station. Maybe someone there knows more about him."

After yelling thank-yous to Mavis, the Muskrats left and were soon heading down the gravel road looking to learn more about a mysteriously malicious man.

CHAPTER 9
Bug Blast

"You! You get out of here! You'll steal from me no more! Your family is not allowed in here!"

As the Muskrats came off the bush trail behind the Station, they heard the high, shrill voice of Mr. Lee, the Station's manager, loudly ejecting someone from the convenience store and gas depot.

"Just turn on the pump, old man!! I got to get to the city."

The Muskrats rounded the corner of the building and stopped as Pearl's older brother, Eddie, stepped up to the smaller, Asian man and poked him in the chest. Eddie was tall and mean looking, with tattooed arms and a huge barrel chest. He was a well-known troublemaker in town and a big reason why Pearl had grown up so tough. His rusty, badly beaten car was hunkered in front of the gas pumps.

When Eddie saw the four young sleuths, he

instinctively looked back at his car. Following his eye, the Muskrats could see Pearl in the passenger's seat and Bug in the back. When she saw them, Pearl's eyebrows rose and she looked shocked. She immediately called to her brother, "Eddie! Let's go. We have enough gas to get out of here."

Eddie glared at the Muskrats and stepped toward the car.

Seeing the source of his troubles was leaving, Mr. Lee threw up his hands, let out an "*Ey-ee-ya!*" and went back into the store.

"Take off, Muskrats!" Eddie waved menacingly at them.

He opened the car door and angrily cursed at his cousin Bug. "We're not paying for you in the city, ya bum!" After his little cousin was ejected, Eddie hopped in. His tires chirped as he stepped on the gas and quickly sped away from the Station.

Samuel looked at his brother and cousins. "That was kind of suspicious."

Atim sounded confused, "Did they take off like that just because of us? Why'd they take off like that?"

Otter was watching Pearl's stranded cousin, who seemed to be deciding if he wanted to attempt going into the Station restaurant or leave altogether.

Bug sniffled and wiped his nose with the back of his hand. He decided to lean heavily against the Station's ice cooler. He was in his usual clothes: a once-white, gray T-shirt and faded, third-hand jeans. The bowl used to define his haircut had been shallow.

"Hey Bug. Where was Eddie taking off to?" Sam tried to sound mildly curious, but not too curious.

"Eddie said they got a big score, and they had to get out of Windy Lake right away. Made me mad! We were supposed to get the crew together. Get some food at the free lunch." Bug shook his head, trying to look tough.

"A big score? So, Pearl didn't even tell you why she left?" Samuel tried to sound credibly incredulous.

Bug stood up straight. "Not even! And we had stuff planned for today."

"Why don't *you* get your crew together?" Chickadee squinted at Bug.

"Uh…what?" Bug frowned.

"Just because Pearl is gone, doesn't mean *you* can't get the gang together, right?" Chickadee pushed a little further.

"Well…*she's* the boss, I guess. I'm not." Bug shrugged and shuffled his feet.

"Well, I think you could be, if Pearl wasn't always pulling you down." Chickadee gathered her hair and flung it over her back.

"Yeah, hey? She is always doing that. Snaggletooth!" Bug looked up at Chickadee. The Muskrats could almost see the gears working inside his head.

"She didn't even tell you where she was going?" Sam circled back.

"The city. That's all Pearl's mom said, anyway. She's my auntie." Bug related the information proudly.

"We know. That's how it works with cousins." Atim could not hide the scorn in his voice.

"What's your problem?" Bug's shields went up.

"Nothing...." The tallest Muskrat and Bug stared at each other for a moment. Bug jerked his chin at Atim. "Got a problem?"

Atim couldn't hold his anger back any longer. "We saw you guys running off with that cooler!" Atim barked it out, a judgmental finger aimed at Bug's chest.

Sam stood in front of his older brother and spoke into his ear. "I thought we agreed that you wouldn't mention that?"

"What cooler?!" Bug stood as tall as he could but was still an inch shorter than Atim. "There was nothing but drinking boxes and wieners and hot dog buns in that cooler. Nobody lost nothing that was worth something. And I got to eat!"

"Don't you care about what visitors think of Windy Lake?" Atim yelled over his brother's shoulder.

"*Pfft*. What has Windy Lake ever done for me?" Bug swaggered. "My family takes care of me!"

"And still, you're hungry," Otter said sadly. His sudden sincerity paused them all.

A slight frown flitted across Bug's features. "Yeah, well. You can't always get what you want." Bug put his head down and slipped between the sleuths. He shuffled across the gravel parking lot, a tiny cloud of dust followed in his wake. "I'm out of here."

"Good move!" Sam said sarcastically as he gave his brother's chest a pat.

Atim cringed and looked disgusted with himself. "I'm sorry! My anger came up. I just couldn't keep it down."

"I lost my cool too." Chickadee shook her head. "I was being mean. And to Bug! He's always been...kind of like a rag doll, you know? Pearl's the one who pushes them around."

"We got to be more like Uncle Levi. We got to be chill, we have to get people to tell us stuff." Sam watched Bug as he walked off into the distance.

"Remember what Yoda said." Otter took on the Jedi Master's voice and bearing. "Clear your mind must be, if you are to find the villains behind this plot."

The Muskrats laughed.

"We need to listen to people's stories to figure this out. We can't let our emotions get in the way. Cool?" Samuel looked around the group.

"We need facts. We can't make bannock without flour," Chickadee chuckled.

The Muskrats all nodded in agreement.

"So...I guess we can cross Pearl and her crew off the

suspect list." Atim flicked the hair out of eyes and raised a finger skyward.

"Why?" Sam scowled as he looked at his brother.

"Well, if Pearl is gone…?"

"Mmm…. Bug said they left because they got a big score. And…if you were going to sell something super unique, where would be the best place to go?" Sam raised an eyebrow at the group.

Atim smacked his forehead. "The city. Of course!"

Chickadee's eyes grew big at the thought. "And she's with Eddie. He's been in more trouble than she has. I bet he'd know who to talk to about selling stolen stuff."

"Yeah. And they took off suddenly, when they saw us," Sam said.

Otter frowned. "You know something else Bug reminded me of? We got to help with lunch today, right?" Otter watched his cousins' reactions. Obviously, it was something they had all forgotten.

"We better get over there!" Chickadee's eyes were wide with shock.

"Denice will kill us!" Sam laughed.

"Last one there is a rotten egg!" Atim yelled as he took off running.

With a cheer, the other Muskrats followed.

★

With the tables and chairs already set up from the day before, the Muskrats had much less work to do to prepare the room for the crowd of Crees cruising in for the lunch crunch. But they were late enough that they all earned a dirty look from Denice along with their aprons. "Put these on. Atim was covered in ketchup by the time you left yesterday."

"Was not!" Atim defended himself with a smile on his face.

"Uncle Levi said the band cops got a call from a lady who thought you'd been in a sword fight," Denice said dryly.

The Muskrats laughed. They all knew what to do, so they got down to it.

The crowd arrived about an hour later. Hungry people, many who had slept in tents the night before, poured into the gym.

The Muskrats slipped into the roles that fit them best. Sam directed traffic, Chickadee tended to Elders, and Atim and Otter, with their quiet smiles, moved between the tables getting chairs and cleaning up. The people were appreciative, but it seemed a weariness had set in throughout the assembled.

As lunch was winding down, the young guard in the buckskin jacket walked in with his family in tow. The long, black hair of their parents was unbraided, but the two little boys had single braids, almost touching their waists. Their mother was a beautiful, young Cree woman, obviously proud of her children. They were well dressed for the weather and cheerful.

"That's the guard that the Elder said wasn't with the others when he showed up." Sam went up to Chickadee and tried not to look like he was pointing out the family as he nodded in their direction.

"The one who was still at his post?" Chickadee asked.

"Yeah. I really want to go talk to him." Sam was pinching his chin, a sure sign that bigger thoughts were forming in his noggin.

"Well, I think the crowd is slowing down. Atim and Otter can keep working. We'll go talk to him. Real quick." Chickadee smiled at her curious cousin.

Sam grinned. "Let's do it!"

Samuel and Chickadee watched the former guard find a seat for his family and, once they were settled, walk away to bring them food from the canteen window.

Sam pulled a garbage bag out of his apron pocket and both he and Chickadee tried to look nonchalant as they wandered closer, picking up enough trash here and there so it wouldn't look like they were making a beeline toward the young father.

"Hey, weren't you at the big teepee this morning?" Sam tried to sound casually curious.

The young man gave them the once-over. "Aren't you a couple of the kids who were there?"

The cousins nodded. "We were wondering if anything weird happened last night?"

"Weird? Not really. It was chilly. I'm still beat from being awake all night."

"Elder Leon said you guys were all gathered together when he arrived in the morning." Sam studied the young man.

"I wasn't. The other guys gathered to do something. I don't know, smoke a cigarette, maybe."

"You don't smoke?" Chickadee smiled at the young man.

"Nope. I only use tobacco in ceremony. Tobacco is medicine, a gift from Creation. You're not supposed to use it just because you want to. There has to be a reason."

Sam wanted to know how serious they had all been about actually being guards. "So, did they leave their post more than once?"

"I don't know. I think we all stayed pretty much in our spots. For me, guarding the bundle was part of ceremony too, right? I was doing my part. But now that I think about it, around three in the morning, I thought I smelled tobacco but, too be honest, I was just concentrating on staying awake." The young man stared at the floor, trying to remember the details of the night. "Yeah, nothing happened until they gathered together just before the Bundle Holder showed up, and, like that Casey guy said, he took off in his truck right away."

"That Casey guy? You two don't sound very close." Chickadee's tone was slightly humorous.

"Eh! We know each other from ceremony. Some Elders and their helpers from Butterfly Narrows came out to Treaty 12 a few years ago. We met then. He knows I'll do what I say. And I stayed in my spot. *They* didn't take it seriously. The bundle is sacred to my people in Treaty 12." The young man shook his head. "This wouldn't have happened if it had stayed in our home territory."

"Well, thanks for talking to us." Sam held out his hand and the young man shook it.

"Why are you two asking about this?" The former guard raised an eyebrow as he asked.

"Our Uncle Levi is the band constable…." Chickadee was going to explain that he had inspired them to be detectives too.

"The guy who took my runners?" He laughed and showed them his feet. Rubber boots, a couple of sizes too large, graced them.

Chickadee and Sam snickered.

With a smile, the young man moved forward in the lineup for the canteen. "Tell your uncle, I want my sneakers back! My pop needs his rubber boots." He turned to the window to pick up meals for his family.

Chickadee and Sam joined Atim and Otter as they cleaned up after the last of the families. Lunch was almost over and only late arrivals, like "Buckskin" and his family, still sat at the tables.

"We're almost done!" Atim beamed.

"And we just spoke with one of the guards from last night." Samuel slapped his brother on the shoulder.

"Really?" Otter's eyes went wide, impressed.

"Yeah, Buckskin. He's over there." Chickadee tried to point with her lips, but the family was sitting too far to the left. Her lips wouldn't stretch that far.

The boys laughed.

"What did he say?" Otter asked.

"Well, we learned not all the guards were from Butterfly Narrows. Buckskin is from Treaty 12. Only knows Casey through ceremony they've done in the past," Sam told them. "Buckskin seemed devoted to protecting the bundle."

"But what if the other boys weren't? And they distracted him on purpose?" Chickadee scowled as she thought it.

"We seem to be gathering more questions, rather than crossing them off our list." Otter's brow furrowed.

"Well, we're getting there! Little by little." Chickadee tried to sound optimistic.

"Detective shows say, if a case is going to be solved, it has to be done in the first forty-eight hours." Samuel looked around the group. "Time is ticking. And if the bundle is already in the city, we only have a few hours of daylight left to prove that it's not in Windy Lake."

CHAPTER 10

A Survey of Suspects

"My family is crushed!"

Brandon Shining Deer sat in the kitchen at Grandpa's scarred, wooden table and explained why he came. "My grandmother is very upset. To her, the bundle is all wrapped up with my great-grandfather and their promise to him. I have never seen her this...confused...and sad. I'd do anything to find the bundle."

Chickadee and Otter tidied up around the men. The tea had just finished steeping, the recently emptied kettle was cooling, and a pot of stew was bubbling on the stove.

"Is Aunt Dee going to be okay?" Chickadee looked at Brandon with sympathetic eyes.

Brandon shook his head. "No. My grandparents are so involved with being Bundle Holders...it's like a piece of her has been lost."

Grandpa grunted as he filled Brandon's cup.

"Something else went missing along with the bundle. The entire Assembly felt off this morning." The old man thought in silence for a moment. "After it was taken, the sunrise ceremony wasn't going to happen, but still…a few of the Elders who should have come, didn't show up."

With a loud creak, the door to the house burst open and Atim and Samuel flew in. "Sorry we're late!" Atim smiled wide.

Sam was bursting with news. "We found out where that Guy guy lives. We bumped into Cousin Mark on the road, and he says Guy lives in the trailer park, just a few doors down from the cop shop."

"Your uncle's office?" Brandon raised an eyebrow.

Grandpa gave Sam the look that said he should be more respectful. "He means the Royal Canadian Mounted Police. Why are you looking for Guy?"

Atim flicked the hair out of his eyes. "Mavis said he hated Crees, and that he bragged he was going to do something to disrupt the Assembly. She figured, if someone in town was going to steal it, Guy would be the guy to do it."

"So, he's on our list of suspects. And now we know where he lives." Sam beamed.

"Don't go putting yourselves in a dangerous situation." Grandpa waggled a stern finger at the Muskrats.

Chickadee went over and took his hand. "We're careful, Grandpa. We check people out before we speak to them."

"And we speak to most people in places where there are a lot of other people close by," Sam assured his Elder.

The Muskrats' grandfather pursed his lips and acknowledged their cautions with an approving gesture and a nod. "So, Muskrats, what else do we know?"

"Well," Chickadee twisted her face in thought. "The usual suspects are out of town...."

"Usual suspects?" Grandpa's brow furrowed.

Sam leaned on the table. "We think we saw a group of people from Windy Lake stealing a cooler from one of the campgrounds." He paused. "We didn't tell Uncle Levi because we don't have any real proof yet."

Atim stepped forward, tapped the table, and interjected loudly. "Bug confessed!"

His brother scoffed. "A cooler isn't the bundle. We need to focus on the case."

"My boys!" Grandpa didn't look up from his tea. The two brothers nodded an apology at each other. Their Elder preferred arguments to stop before they led to harsh words.

Chickadee began to describe their other line of investigation. "We learned that not all the guards who were watching the bundle were from Butterfly Narrows. One guy, we call him Buckskin, is from Treaty 12. And he wasn't too impressed with how the other boys handled the job."

Brandon nodded. "He's from the Treaty 12 area. Just

not our community. Been to ceremony with him a few times."

"He seems like a good guy. I don't think he did anything. He loves the bundle." Chickadee nodded confidently at her assessment.

"I wouldn't think so either," Brandon told the group.

"That leaves the other three to cross off the list." Atim opened the fridge and stuck his head inside.

"Do you figure one of them took it?" Brandon looked down at the table, obviously contemplating the idea.

"We don't know." Otter was standing behind the other Muskrats leaning against the kitchen counter.

"When did you get there, Brandon?" Sam asked.

"I arrived with my grandfather. He went into the teepee. I was talking to the guards…."

"All of them?" Sam's eyebrows raised.

"Well, three of them. One was standing at the back still…watching the bush."

"The guy in the buckskin?" Chickadee ventured.

"Mhmm." Brandon took a sip of his tea.

"What about the Elder?" Otter almost whispered it.

Grandpa sat up straight. "What do you mean…the Elder?"

"Well…the Elder from Butterfly Narrows was pretty upset with…everything. The big teepee is probably his, right? Could he be so angry that…he stole the bundle?"

"That is a terrible charge, Otter." Grandfather stared

at his grandson for a moment. "And it wouldn't make sense. It wouldn't be his treaty's bundle! What value would it have to him?" Grandpa's long hair danced as he shook his head.

Sam looked at his Elder as he spoke. "Could he have wanted Windy Lake's Cree Assembly to fail?"

At that, Grandpa thought a moment. He sounded disappointed as he spoke. "If he took my joke as disrespectful...stealing the bundle would be a very harsh reaction. But I don't know the man well enough to know if he could do such a thing."

"Then we have to put him on the list," Sam said quietly.

Grandpa paused, then nodded. "We would have to be very careful with that one. If we accuse an Elder of doing something so...terrible, and he didn't do it, that would be very bad for the entire Cree Nation."

"I never thought of that," Atim admitted.

Sam sighed heavily. "Grandpa...I'm worried about talking to him...because I kicked the pipes, and his was there."

Grandpa's face scrunched as he tried to figure out what his grandson was talking about. Finally, coming across the memory, he broke into laugher and slapped his knee. "Oh yes! I forgot about that. Oh, your face...!" Grandpa giggled uncontrollably, rocking back and forth.

Sam chuckled, relieved that his Elder hadn't harbored

anger over the accidental sacrilege. "I'm so sorry, Grandpa. I didn't mean to do it. I was carrying that big pot of stew...."

"It's all right, my boy." His grandfather held up one hand as the other was placed on his chest, trying to hold in the laughter. "We could see you were sorry as soon as you kicked the Grandfathers."

"Grandfathers?" Sam's curiosity trumped his chuckles.

"Our sacred pipes are alive. They have spirit. And so, we honor them by calling them 'Grandfathers'—teachers, from whom so much goodness flows."

"Do you think the Elder from Butterfly Narrows will forgive me for kicking his pipe?"

"I don't know. I forgive you, because I saw your regret immediately and I knew you were sorry. That goes for the Elders around me, too." Grandpa paused thoughtfully. He stared at the floor. "But for something like this, you will have to make amends to each one you've wronged. You were working for the ceremony, and it was an accident, so no one should be too harsh on you. But it is up to them to measure the weight of your disrespect. And they have a right to set the toll for resolving the damage." Grandpa wasn't giggling anymore. He was looking Samuel in the eyes, his wrinkled face calm and serious.

Everyone else listened to the exchange quietly.

Sam was both warmed and worried by his grandfather's words. "I want to do what's right."

Grandpa nodded. "Good, my son. That means you have some road to walk to make things right." His Elder continued. "It's good to close the circles we start. Things can get very out of balance if left unaddressed."

They all sat in silence for a moment.

Brandon shook his head, worried. "The bundle kept a balance. I don't know what will happen if it gets taken out of the Treaty 12 circle…forever. I'm not sure how that would ripple out. It would certainly change my people." Brandon's face fell. "We have to get it back. It's tearing my grandparents apart."

The outside door creaked open and a chilly wind rushed in. Uncle Levi pushed it closed with one strong arm. He hung his Windy Lake band constable cap on a hook and took off his boots. After removing his footwear, he put the cap back on.

"We're just talking about the bundle, my son." The old man raised his voice so Uncle Levi could hear him.

"Well, Pop. Been looking at the tracks around the tee-pee. Looks like someone went under the side wall. They were small, cowboy boots, probably."

"Cowboy boots?" Chickadee raised her eyebrows.

"Yeah, you could see the pointy toe where it cut into the mud. They must have crawled under the canvas when the guards weren't looking."

"Or when the guards were letting them through…." Atim let the thought hang in the air.

"What do you mean?" Uncle Levi was curious.

Sam explained. "Well, we figured, if the guards didn't take it themselves, maybe they knew someone who wanted to take it and just looked the other way." Sam raised his palms skyward and shrugged. "It's just a…possibility… one idea we're following."

Uncle Levi lifted his cap and scratched his head thoughtfully. He put the cap back on. "Be careful who you talk to about that. You can't go throwing accusations everywhere. You Muskrats will get hurt if you get the wrong people angry…and I might not be there to help." Uncle Levi's voice was filled with caution.

"We'll watch ourselves." Chickadee promised, as her cousins nodded seriously.

Uncle Levi frowned, rubbed his jaw, and studied them. "Those boys still have to come pick up their shoes. I can ask them about it then."

"Why aren't the RCMP helping?" Brandon wanted to know.

Uncle Levi writhed slightly as he wrestled out something he didn't want to say. "We won't get much help from them. I spoke to them earlier. It seems the bundle is only valuable to us Cree. When I told the RCMP about it, they acted like it wasn't more alarming than someone shoplifting from the co-op."

"What?" Brandon almost stood up.

Grandpa snorted and scoffed. "The more valuable

something is, the more people they'll send to find it, but there is no gold in the bundle."

Uncle Levi nodded. "They'll keep an eye out, for sure. But they ain't bringing out the CSI team. We're mostly on our own."

Brandon held his head in his hands, looking down at the table. "We got to figure this out. We *have* to get the bundle back."

"You Muskrats." Grandpa pointed at each of the kids. He obviously had an idea. "We don't have any evidence that the Elder from Butterfly Narrows is involved. I doubt he'll be expecting questions from kids."

Uncle Levi shook his head at his father. "So, you want them to interrogate this Elder?"

"Not interrogate...tickle a little." Grandpa smiled. "These Muskrats can read his heart. They can poke where you and I dare not joke." The old man chuckled at his play on words.

Uncle Levi let out a lungful of air through pursed lips, obviously uncomfortable with the idea.

Grandpa reached across the table and grasp his son's forearm. "I am not sending them into battle. There is an Elders' dinner tomorrow at the Cultural Camp."

Grandpa gestured toward Sam and Chickadee. "These Muskrats can take a measure of his heart. See if he is angry with Windy Lake, or just me. Sometimes old warriors will brag to children."

Uncle Levi shook his head but, eventually, conceded. "All right. I can't stop you from talking to people. Just be careful. And, if you find out anything incriminating, you do not say anything to anyone. Just come talk to me, okay?"

The Muskrats smiled and nodded.

"Okay." Uncle Levi studied them out of the corner of his eye. "I suspect this will lead to trouble."

CHAPTER 11
Bunts and Bluster

"That bundle wouldn't have been hard to take, eh! Not for a sneaky Métis-Mohawk and only a coupl'a sleepy Crees to get past. If I did it, I'd be going about my business as usual, not doing anything weird that would get the cops suspicious, ya know?"

Samuel, Chickadee, and Otter sat in the bleachers of the Windy Lake Baseball Diamonds waiting for the start of Atim's first softball game of the day. Just by chance, one of their prime suspects was sitting in the bleachers spouting off in heavily accented English.

During the adult baseball game that had just ended, Guy had regaled his buddies, as well as anyone within earshot, with tale after tale of his implausible life. Throughout it all, his monologue was scattered with French expressions, put-downs against the local culture, climate, nightlife, and people. Even though the Muskrats' ears had trouble catching up to his French accent, it didn't take much sleuthing to understand he had a low opinion of just about everything...except himself.

"The Mohawks were living in longhouses while those silly Cree were still movin' around like a bunch of drifters. Who cares what they call sacred?" Guy obviously didn't care who heard him. He looked like a brown-haired imp. A spikey mop sat atop his head and he wore a green jacket with a denim vest on top.

Chickadee shifted in her chair. Finally, she hissed, "What a jerk! Sounds like he's just saying he didn't do it, *because* he did it!"

Sam shook his head. "Remember what happened with Bug? We can't judge a guy just because we think he's a jerk. That's not an investigation, anyway."

Chickadee shrugged.

Otter leaned in. "We can't let our feelings get in the way of facts, right?"

Samuel smiled at his cousin. "Right."

Guy had continued unabated. "I figure something like that, if you find the right buyer, it could go for a pretty penny."

"Hey Guy, you better watch what you say. The Mighty Muskrats are here." One of Guy's friends mockingly threw a thumb in the young sleuths' direction. "Their uncle is the chief Indian cop."

"Who's that?" Guy sat up straight and looked over at

the four cousins. "You kids going to tell on me, eh?" The Frenchman laughed. "Hey, you kiddies, did you hear me?"

The Mighty Muskrats tried hard to pretend they did not.

A local mom sitting close to Guy's group came to their rescue. Her hefty bulk leaned forward, an early-morning Coke in hand. "Quiet, Guy. Leave those kids alone. They're good kids. Probably nothing like you were when you were little."

"Aww, my love. I'm just having a little fun." Guy tried to take the mom's free hand, but she smacked his away.

"Just keep your sticky fingers to yourself, Mr. Guy." She yelled over to the Muskrats. "Don't worry about Guy. He's just being a jerk."

Sam raised an eyebrow and looked at his cousins.

Chickadee stole a look in Guy's direction, and her face was conflicted as she whispered. "I don't know. He says so many things, who knows what's true and what's just hot air?"

Guy and his friends stood and began to make their way down the bleachers.

With much noise and bluster, the Frenchman walked out along the trail at the bottom of the stands.

Otter nodded in their suspect's direction. "Check out his feet."

"Cowboy boots! Does that mean it's him?" Chickadee whispered, wide-eyed.

"Well…that makes it a little more likely." Sam's brow furrowed as he pondered the new information. "But it's not hard evidence yet. It doesn't prove it was him. Lots of people wear cowboy boots. We'd have to get Uncle Levi to compare the footprints, I guess."

"What do we do now?" Chickadee raised her palms skyward.

"Grandpa wants us to go to the Elders' fish fry at the Cultural Camp later." Otter squinted in the sun.

Samuel tapped a pointed finger against his lips. "I would like to track down at least one of the other teepee guards from the other night."

"So, we still have plenty to do." Chickadee leaned back against the bleacher just above theirs.

The trio watched the most athletic of the Muskrats lead the Windy Lake teen softball team to another victory. After the handshake between teams, and pats on the back from his team members, Atim ran over to the bleachers to meet his brother and cousins.

As they made their way from the diamond and into the parking lot, Samuel filled Atim in on the incident in the stands.

"That Guy guy sure is a loudmouth," he said.

"We'll need to find out more about him." Chickadee pulled back her long, black hair so it hung down her back.

"If you want to know more about me, just ask." Guy

stepped from between two parked trucks. One of his friends walked around from the other side.

The Muskrats were caught between the men.

"You kids going to tell your cop uncle what I said?" Guy's chuckle was slightly menacing.

Sam kept his face as emotionless as possible but inside he was freaking out. "Nothing you said proves you even touched the bundle."

Guy snorted. He looked Samuel over, impressed. "Right."

"Weren't you just talking, what do you say, hypothetically?" Atim flicked the hair out of his eyes.

Guy squinted and looked at the Muskrats out of the side of his eye. "Yeah, I was. That's…just what I wanted to hear. Let's keep it that way." He raised an eyebrow and nodded at the Muskrats to suggest he expected compliance.

As Guy turned back to one of the trucks, Chickadee pointed at his blue and gray cowboy boots. "Nice boots."

He turned back. With a looked he appraised Chickadee's sincerity.

"I mean it." Chickadee tried to sound like one of the women who sold boots on the Home Shopping Channel. "They're a nice pattern, from what I can see below the hem of your jeans, and the boots are the kind of gray that would go with a lot of different colors and outfits. You'd never need to take them off."

Charmed, Guy turned back and lifted his jean leg

to reveal more of the patterned boot. "I just came back from out West. I bought them in cowboy country. Haven't worn anything else since."

"I like nice footwear." Chickadee smiled up at the man.

Guy looked down at her ragged shoes. Chickadee would wear her favorite sneakers until they hung in tatters and eventually dissolved with age.

When Guy looked up, he reassessed the Muskrats through a suspicious side-eye. "I don't know if you kids are for real or not, but if the cops come my way, I'll know who sent them. Understand?"

The Muskrats nodded and started walking away.

The man stared aggressively at the young sleuths as he got into his truck. With spinning wheels, the Muskrats' suspect sent a cloud of gravel and dust in their direction. They could hear the men laughing over the roar of the engine.

✦

"I still want to stop by the guest camp and see if we can bump into one of the failed bundle guards." Sam stared at the road as he spoke.

Atim loped along beside his brother. "It *is* on the way and they're the one group we haven't really spoken to yet."

With a shout, the boys followed after Chickadee, smiles on their faces. It didn't take long to get to the guest camp where they knew the Shining Deers stayed, and, they believed, where a few of the failed guards camped.

The camp had been set up in a small field, one side hedged in by the road and then the forest, while the opposite edge was a fairly steep slope leading down to the lake. The farther the sleuths walked down the temporary lane, the deeper and darker the shade thrown by the forest. The campgrounds were alive with activity. Families of all sizes going to and fro from friendly visits and Assembly events.

Unlike the rest of the temporary neighborhood, the Shining Deer camp was lonely and quiet as the Muskrats walked past. The lights were off in the RV. No cook fire was evident. A neglected picnic table stoically took up space in the center of the lot.

"Yeesh. Is anyone in there?" Atim stood on his tippy toes to look farther into the camp and RV.

"Little blue car is gone." Sam motioned to the empty space.

"That's Aunt Dee's." A sad frown stretched between Chickadee's freckled cheeks.

"Brandon said they were really hurting from the bundle being stolen," Otter remarked with a shake of his head. The Muskrats marched on quietly.

The other camps were bustling with life. The young detectives didn't know exactly where the guards were parked, but they nonchalantly checked out each family they passed.

Almost at the end of the grounds, a couple of familiar faces looked back as the Muskrats walked by.

"Tansi!" Sam waved at the two families, saying hello.

The two former guards put down what they were doing and walked toward the road, eyeing the Muskrats suspiciously. The taller one had long hair and wore a thick flannel shirt over a faded, black AC/DC T-shirt. The shorter man looked like he might have been a soldier with camouflage pants, a green T-shirt, and an army of muscles.

Sam pointed at their shoes. "I see you got your sneakers back."

The young men glanced down at their feet. By the time they looked up, they were laughing. The taller of the two lip-pointed at the Muskrats. "You were the kids at the teepee the other morning."

"Yeah. That's us." Atim gestured at the rest of his troops. "This is my brother Sam, and my cousins, Chickadee and Otter."

"We were wondering if we could ask you some questions." Sam tried to sound friendly.

The young men looked at each other and shrugged. "Why not? Nothing really to tell. We sat out there, each in our corner, most of the night."

"Most of the night?" Atim's brow furrowed. "You guys didn't move at all? Not even to pee?"

The former guard suddenly looked chagrined. "Well, yeah. We didn't stand like statues all night."

"When we got there, you were all standing in a clump," Otter commented.

"Yeah, Casey's phone finally downloaded this video of the hockey game. We were all watching it when you guys showed up. Just bad timing, I guess."

"You weren't smoking?" Chickadee wrinkled her nose.

The young men shook their heads. The short one finally spoke. "We only smoke during ceremony. Cigarettes are gross."

"But you did say there was another time you got together…." Sam was squinting up at the man.

"Well, yeah…." The tall one again looked like he had a secret he didn't want to tell.

Snickering, the shorter man gave him a playful push. "Brave Heart here thought he heard a ghost."

"Well…I heard something that these guys didn't hear." The tall guard shook his head, chuckling. "They think it was just my imagination."

"What did it sound like?" Otter asked.

The taller guard shook his head. "Could have been a bird, I guess, but it made a noise…like someone crying."

The "soldier" laughed openly at his friend. "He came running over to my side of the teepee and wouldn't leave. Casey had to come and convince him to go back. Took a while."

The tall man smirked. "Ahh…I guess it was just something in the bush. It did freak me out, I admit. But other than that, there was nothing, it was just a cold and dark night."

Otter suddenly piped up. "No visitors?"

The two men looked at each other. The taller man shook his head. The shorter one stared at the ground. Obviously, something was on his mind.

Sam and the other Muskrats could see the information trying to wiggle out of the man. They waited. A tense silence grew long.

When the itch was too much, the shorter man spoke. "There was a visitor. We didn't think of it before, but shortly after everyone left...one of the Elders from Butterfly Narrows did go into the teepee."

"But it's his teepee, and he said he was just getting some of his things." The taller man's voice was slightly pleading. "We forgot about it, he was in and out so quick, and it was so soon after our shift started."

"Was it the Elder who looks...." Otter was eager to ask about his suspicions but had no way of referring to the Butterfly Narrows Elder, other than his features.

The soldier chuckled. "Was it the Elder who looks like a toad? Yeah. We call him Toad Man when we're feeling mean."

Otter smiled, happy he didn't have to say it.

The taller man seemed more willing to speak, once the cat was out of the bag.

"His name is Elder Eugene Lone Man. He's a strict

guy when it comes to ceremony. You don't want to be caught being disrespectful around him!"

"We should tell the band constable we remembered something new, hey?" The soldier looked at the Muskrats.

The young detectives nodded. After quick good-byes, the four of them took their fresh information down the road.

"The old toad *did* go into the teepee after everyone left!" Atim fist punched the air.

"Elder Lone Man...," Otter cautioned.

Sam pinched his chin, thoughtfully. "We'll be speaking with that Elder at the dinner later tonight. We better figure out what we're going to say. We don't want to pull apart the entire Cree Nation!"

CHAPTER 12
Angry Elder

"You're the one that kicked my pipe!"

Sam froze when he heard the words. He turned around slowly.

Sitting by the fire with a plate of fish, potatoes, creamed corn, and a square of bannock balanced on the side was the Toad Man, aka Elder Eugene Lone Man. An ancient baseball cap shaded glasses that were like framed satellite dishes, and faded jeans covered legs so spindly they appeared unlikely to carry their burden.

Whatever plan the Muskrats had to gather information from the Butterfly Lake Elder fluttered out the window.

At Grandpa's request, they had hopped in a boat and made their way to the Cultural Camp to volunteer for the Elders' Dinner in the hope they could speak to Elder Lone Man. The Muskrats were quickly assigned to handing out the pickerel and hunks of bannock to the old ones gathered around the campfire that crackled in the midst of a circle of teepees.

After hearing the Elder's challenge, Atim and Chickadee each dared a glance with wide eyes but continued to hand out food.

Otter stopped beside Sam, knowing his cousin might need some moral support.

"I am...." Samuel paused, uncertain if respect demanded that he speak first. "I'm really sorry. I was carrying that big pot...."

The Elder frowned and shook his head. "My pipe is sacred to me. And you kicked it. In ceremony, no less...."

Sam stepped closer, wanting to show the man he was willing to listen. "I didn't do it on purpose. I was working for the ceremony—"

"Enough!" The Elder was so agitated he almost bounced on the stump he sat on. "Enough excuses! You were disrespectful."

Sam sighed. "I was, Elder." He spread out his hands. "How can I make it up to you?" Samuel felt strengthened with Otter standing right beside him, listening to the exchange.

The Elder was quiet for a moment, obviously, trying to get the better of his anger. "I take ceremony seriously. And it sounded like you were trying to brush away your responsibilities."

Samuel shook his head. "No. I just wanted you to understand that I didn't do it on purpose but I know I did it."

The Elder seemed to shake off his earlier attitude. Suddenly, a twinkle appeared in his eye and his frog-like mouth peeled back in the widest grin that Sam had ever seen. Elder Lone Man's gleaming white teeth were a wall of mirth. "You should have seen your face when it first happened." The old man slapped his knee and laughed, almost losing his plate.

Sam shrugged. "I've been told. The other Elders are already teasing me about it."

The old man's chuckles continued. "It'll take you a while to live that one down. Here, sit here, you boys." The old man motioned to two nearby stumps and then turned back to his food.

Samuel and Otter went over to the wooden seats and sat down, leaning forward with their elbows on their knees. They sat in silence as Elder Lone Man shoveled.

Finally, Sam took a stab at small talk. "We're from Windy Lake. Our grandfather is—"

"I know what family you're from." The Elder studied them over the edge of his plate. "You're the kids they call The Mighty Muskrats."

The boys smiled and nodded.

The old man flashed his ear-to-ear grin. "Funny name." He took a bite of battered fish, chewing away his smile. With his fork, he gestured toward Otter. "Your grandfather thinks he's funny."

Otter's eyes grew wide. He nodded, his cute face strained, lips pressed tightly together.

"*Humph!*" The Elder was thoughtful as he scooped more from his dinner.

"You know how you can pay me back for kicking my pipe?" The Elder looked off into the early evening sky.

Sam shook his head, apprehensive. Otter was curious.

"I want you to find that bundle." He went back to eating.

Sam and Otter wanted to hear more. It was killing Sam to keep quiet, but he knew if he let the silence sit long enough, the Elder would eventually put something into it.

The Elder swallowed, paused, then sighed before he spoke. "We need to bring our people together. We need to end our gathering in a good way." The Elder threw in another spoonful.

"Really?" Sam raised his eyebrows under his crew-cut hair.

"Really. There is more to this Assembly than just our personal problems." Elder Lone Man paused and looked at Sam and then settled on Otter. "That's why…I want you to do something else…." The Elder stared at his shoes for a moment.

As the lull stretched on, the boys shifted uncomfortably.

"In Butterfly Lake, we watched…we watched as other communities had their traditions stripped, had their beliefs mixed with those of the Settlers. My grandfathers decided to keep our ceremony pure. To maintain the old ways of doing things as much as possible. So, we hid them." The Elder seemed to be looking back into his family history as he focused on the distant horizon. "I know there are hungry people now. I know there are people who want to relearn their traditions. But in Butterfly Lake, we were given the chance to protect what we have. The right way of doing the old ways."

The boys nodded with the old man. They didn't look him in the eye, they just listened, waiting for more teachings to download.

"I know that now, there are lodges letting boys from gangs take part in ceremony—some of our most sacred ceremonies. Hoping to, I don't know, jump-start them." The old man motioned like he was using the paddles of a defibrillator, and an electric shock was passing into his patient. "To zap them back into the culture, electrify their desire to leave the cold and come under the blanket." He shook his head. "It rarely works. And I don't agree with it."

Hungry for teachings, Samuel's brow furrowed, he crossed his arms. Steeped in tradition, Otter nodded along with the Elder.

"But can someone work their way into the most

sacred ceremonies, even if they were born in the city and are just learning them now?" Sam's voice held a touch of desperation.

The Elder's lips pursed. He nodded. "Let me put that a better way. You can't take someone from step one right to step ten. They need to earn each step. They're not just simple...," the Elder was frustrated at his loss of words, "chores. You're not just doing things to earn a badge. The vision quest, the warrior's dance, joining a society, preparation for the sundance...these are not just about memorizing protocols and steps, they must be *lived*. The ideas and experience must seep into your memories and muscles." Elder Lone Man was getting excited. He was obviously passionate about the subject.

Seeing Sam and Otter had gotten over the hard part of the conversation with the Butterfly Lake Elder, Atim and Chickadee joined them.

The old man nodded a welcome but continued to speak to the two boys. "That's why we do not allow pictures at ceremony. It is the experience that is the message. And snapshots do not carry that spirit. They do not capture the ceremony completely in a way that would give the person seeing it the entire teaching in their heart, in their mind, in their spirt, and even in their muscles and sinews that experiencing it would."

The four Muskrats waited respectfully in case Elder Lone Man wanted to speak again.

He chuckled. "So, what was I saying? Everyone, even the young men we want to save, must experience the teachings and challenges of each step. We can't just zap them to step ten and hope their ceremonial heart will start beating." Elder Lone Man sighed. "Anyway…what I'm trying to say is…sometimes it is hard to put aside our hurt feelings. But the group is always more important than the…." The Elder slapped his knee and laughed. "The group is always more important than the lone man." He smiled at his own joke.

Otter and Samuel grinned back.

"So, I want you to tell your grandfather that bygones be bygones and things are fine between us. Okay?"

The Muskrats beamed, then nodded their good-byes to Elder Lone Man.

★

"Do we strike him off the list?" Sam asked.

The Muskrats had gathered in front of the cookhouse and out of earshot of anyone else to discuss what had just happened.

Atim scoffed. "What about 'We can't let our feelings get in the way of facts?' Just because you like him now, we strike him off the list?"

Sam stared at the ground for a while and shook his head. "No, I guess not."

"But you don't think it was it him?" Chickadee squinted at Sam, then Otter. They shook their heads.

Chickadee put her hands on her hips. "Why not?"

Otter lifted an eyebrow and held up his index finger. "First, he asked for us to *find* the bundle—"

"Could have been to set us off the scent," Atim interrupted.

Otter shot him a skeptical glance and then lifted another finger. "Two, he cares too much about ceremony."

"What does that mean?" Atim raised his eyebrows.

Otter's face twisted as he thought. "Given what he said about experience and ceremony, I just think the bundle…wouldn't be from his people's history, his people's ceremonies, so it wouldn't be his to take. A bundle from his people would be super important, but a bundle from other people's history? It just wouldn't…be worth the trouble to take…."

Chickadee made a face like she was judging Otter's argument, waved her hand back and forth, and then looked to Samuel for his answer.

Sam pressed his lips together and then blew out a lungful of air, scratched his head, and looked up at the sky. Right now, it was just a feeling that the old man had nothing to do with the missing bundle, but Sam couldn't say he had anything but a hunch. He looked over at Elder Lone Man, still sitting by the fire. The Elder now seemed more like a laughing Kermit the Frog than an angry toad.

The old man was rocking back and forth as he guffawed, his legs kicked off the ground as he leaned back.

"It's his feet," Sam announced suddenly.

"His feet?" Atim and Chickadee voiced together. All the sleuths took a quick glance at Elder Lone Man.

"Moccasins," Otter whispered.

"Doesn't mean it wasn't him," Atim said.

"But it makes him a little less likely," Sam responded. "The Elder is off my list...for now."

Atim shrugged and then shook his head. "He ain't off mine."

"We have to tell Grandpa what we heard, either way." Chickadee looked around for their grandfather. He was engrossed in conversation with some old friends from far away. "Maybe we can wait until morning."

"We need more info. What we're finding out just isn't enough to unravel things." Sam sounded frustrated.

"Where's Pearl?" Otter's eyebrows rippled with the question.

"We still don't know if she could have taken it, wherever she disappeared to." Chickadee pursed her lips.

Sam cringed as he spoke. "But if she did take it...it will be sold and gone by now. Probably lost forever."

CHAPTER 13

Time, Treaty, and Two Canoes

"We're running out of leads...and the forty-eight hours when we are most likely to find the stolen bundle is done." Samuel was frustrated.

The Muskrats had just finished doing morning chores for Grandpa and now discussed the case of the burgled bundle with their band constable uncle and their Elder.

"Really? Who have the Muskrats crossed off their list?" Uncle Levi shifted his large weight slightly in his chair as he turned to look at Sam.

The young sleuths couldn't help but notice their uncle's tone was genuine and interested.

"Well...we haven't spoken to Casey yet, but given what you said about cowboy boots, it is unlikely the guards took it." Sam ticked off three fingers.

"I wondered if the angry Elder from Butterfly Narrows stole it." Otter's elfin face was serious. "But we spoke to

Elder Lone Man, and we no longer think he did it. He just...cares about ceremony too much to see the bundle as having value to him and his people. It's not from their land...their history."

Grandpa had been unusually quiet this morning, his voice was grave as he spoke. "That sounds like it should. It was hard to hold the idea that a Knowledge Keeper would do that, even if he was angry with me."

Samuel nodded. "You know Grandpa, he's just as worried about Cree unity as you are. He told us to tell you that he's over his anger and he's putting it in the past."

Grandpa allowed himself a subtle grin. "I will have to speak to him. Maybe we can work together to pull the Assembly out of this...depression."

"There is one group of people that took off the morning the bundle was stolen. We haven't spoken to them yet." Atim's voice had a slight edge to it.

Uncle Levi noticed. "Who is that?"

"We don't have any evidence they did anything," Sam cautioned his brother.

"We know they steal stuff!" Atim shot back.

"The usual suspects, hey?" Uncle Levi frowned. "We've been looking into those too. Who are you talking about?"

Samuel's face scrunched and looked conflicted. The other Muskrats waited for him to say something, but Atim was eager to speak for himself.

"Do we have to tell you? We don't really have any evidence." Sam looked at his Uncle.

Atim couldn't hold it in anymore. "Bug basically confessed to stealing the cooler!!"

Sam raised his eyebrows at his brother and shook his head.

Uncle Levi knew Windy Lake well. "So...Pearl's crew? They're mostly crimes-of-opportunity types. Not sure they have the brains to pull something like this off."

"What do you mean by crimes of opportunity?" Chickadee placed a bowl of blueberries on the table as she asked the question.

Uncle Levi took off his cap, scratched his head through his slightly graying hair, and then replaced the cap. "Well...people do crimes for different reasons. Crimes of opportunity are when someone sees something in the moment...like a cooler being left unattended. So, they grab it. But there are other motivations: passion, revenge, personal benefit. Those are all reasons someone might commit a crime."

"Hmmm...I guess we've struck off revenge with our talk with Elder Lone Man." Otter pursed his lips.

"I think most of those wouldn't apply to the bundle. The person who took it probably thought it had cash value," Uncle Levi assured them. "I wouldn't be surprised if Pearl's crew thought it was valuable, but I can't see them braving the guards to get it."

"What about her older brother, Eddie? He took off with her to the city," Atim ventured.

"Hmmm…he's a little more criminally minded. I'll be keeping an eye out for both of them."

"What happens if they did take it and are now in the city?" Atim asked.

Uncle Levi sighed. "Not sure. It could be gone, I guess."

"What about Guy?" Chickadee scowled as she thought about the man. "Mavis said he was her first suspect. He hates Neechies, and we heard him speculating what he would do if he stole the bundle."

Uncle Levi snorted. "Guy? He's a loudmouth for sure. Mavis thinks it could be him, hey?"

"He wears cowboy boots. And he's small," Samuel stated matter-of-factly. "But that doesn't really mean any-thing, does it?"

Uncle Levi snorted. "You know how many people wear cowboy boots?"

Everyone chuckled.

"Sooo…if a Canadian stole a treaty bundle, does that mean the treaty is broken?" Atim asked.

"Good question!" Sam fist bumped his brother.

The adults chuckled.

Grandpa shifted in his seat. "No, a Canadian stealing a treaty bundle would not end the treaty, but it would be a sad thing. Remember, I said that treaties were made between nations, so they could only be broken by a nation. It's not possible for an individual."

Uncle Levi nodded in agreement. "As a lawman, I like the two canoes teaching about treaty-making. It was given to me by a Mohawk from out East."

"Guy says he's part Mohawk, that's why he says he's Métis," Chickadee blurted.

"Guy's a Frenchman. Being Métis doesn't mean you have a little bit of Indian blood. I bet he couldn't even name his Mohawk ancestor, if there actually is one."

"Tapwe, that's true," Grandpa agreed with his son. The old man chuckled. "When you think about it, nine months after any two people meet each other, there could be mixed-bloods. A little bit of Indian blood in you does not a nation make. The Métis are a nation. That's what's indigenous to Canada...that nation and culture." Grandpa shrugged a shoulder. "Or so the argument goes."

Uncle Levi agreed with his father.

"Uncle, you were saying something about two canoes before Chickadee brought up Guy again," Sam said.

"Oh yeah...the two canoes. Well, my Mohawk buddy said that, in their teachings, their treaty with the Settlers was explained through a story about two separate peoples in two separate canoes, deciding to travel down the river of history together. Each canoe would be filled with the law, culture, language, and beliefs of the people within it. And the people from one canoe would not try to interfere with the other, and versa-vicey. Instead, they would journey through time together, side by side."

"But that's not what happened. The Settlers did interfere with us, didn't they?" Atim's face was serious.

"Yes, they did." Uncle Levi nodded sadly.

Grandpa sighed and shook his head. "They eroded our laws, our lands, our governance systems through their law, backed up by their police. And they damaged our families and our languages and cultures through things like Residential Schools and the Scoops."

"That's what took your little sister, Auntie Charlotte." Chickadee looked sadly at her grandfather.

His eyes filled with sorrow. "And we never saw her again."

The band constable took a handful of berries and threw them into his mouth. "Hopefully, things are changing." After a chew and a swallow, he continued. "I was at a conference a couple of years ago. This professor from the University of Victoria was there talking about a new program they had to revitalize traditional law. It's exciting: they take old stories and legends, boil them down to the foundation of ideas and beliefs that are inside them, and then they use those foundations to build new law. Law that works in today's world and comes directly from the culture and beliefs of that First Nation."

Sam's eyes were big. "I want to know more about that!!"

"It's pretty cool stuff. She was a super-smart lady. I think I had a crush on her for a while."

"Ever sick, Uncle." Chickadee gave her uncle a playful punch on the shoulder.

Her uncle laughed. "I never did anything. Too shy. Just admired her mind and passion from afar." Uncle Levi shifted his weight and cleared his throat. "I got to hit the road, but listen. Guy was probably just getting off work when you saw him the other morning. He works nights. I know Guy's boss. I'll ask him if Guy was working that night."

"That would be great, Uncle. Then we could cross him off our suspect list." Sam and the other Muskrats nodded with appreciation.

"Okay. Well, now that we've spoken about the suspects, I want you to go check on the Shining Deer camp." Grandpa waved at the Muskrats. "My friends Leon and Dee are having a hard time of it with the bundle missing. I want you to see if there are any chores they need doing."

"No problem, Grandpa. We can head down there now." Otter patted his Elder's shoulder.

"It will be good to see Aunt Dee again. I hope she's okay." Chickadee's freckled face was filled with concern.

"I want to go to the Station and see if we can find any word on Pearl." Sam pinched his chin thoughtfully. "The forty-eight hours are up."

"Well…." Uncle Levi stood and hitched up his belt. "I

never really held to that forty-eight hours thing, anyway. Small towns aren't the city. I think our real deadline is the end of the Assembly. Once everyone goes home, it will be almost impossible to figure out who took the missing bundle."

CHAPTER 14

Family Fights and False Memories

"Let's get to their campsite quick, my arms are killing me." Samuel was carrying wood for the Shining Deers' fire, just like his brother, Atim, and cousin Otter.

"We're only a couple of spots away." Atim took some firewood off Sam's armload and placed it on his own.

The Shining Deer camp was quiet. Brandon sat at the picnic table looking dejected. He smiled weakly at the Muskrats. "Any news of the bundle?"

Chickadee shook her head. "Sorry, no."

The sound of logs hitting the ground, was followed by groans from the other Muskrats as they dropped their loads, then rubbed their muscles.

Brandon gave a nod to each of them in appreciation. "Thanks for the wood."

Otter smiled as he brushed the woodchips off his clothes. "It's all good."

"My grandparents just had a huge argument. They're in the camper. My grandma is getting ready to leave." Brandon rubbed his forehead.

Chickadee sat down beside him and placed a compassionate hand on his back. "Was it about the bundle?"

"What else? She said the stress was hurting her."

The Muskrats shared surprised looks.

Suddenly, the screen door of the RV opened and slammed shut. Aunt Dee descended its few steps and pulled her car keys from her purse. She was obviously deep within her own thinking because she didn't seem to notice the Muskrats until Chickadee said hello.

Aunt Dee looked up, slightly startled and obviously distraught. "Oh, hello Chickadee, boys. I'm just off to pick up some of the things that were in the big teepee with the bundle...and then get something to calm my nerves."

"It's okay, Aunt Dee." Chickadee's freckled face broke into a kind smile. "Grandpa told us to bring you some wood."

Absentmindedly, the older woman looked at the dumped logs. "That's good. Now Brandon won't have to do it." She looked back at the RV, then at her grandson. "Brandon, you be sure to help your grandfather." Her sad eyes and furrowed brow showed she meant more than just camp chores.

"I will, Grandma." Brandon filled his voice with compassion. He then whispered to Muskrats, "Could someone go with her? She's far from home, and I don't want her to be alone."

Aunt Dee was unlocking the door of the little blue car. Chickadee gave Atim a nudge. When he looked at her, Chickadee raised her eyebrows and nodded her chin toward Aunt Dee.

Atim shook his head. He had never really had a conversation with Aunt Dee before and didn't know what to say once he was alone with her.

Chickadee's face took on a stern look, she gave him another nudge, and she strongly lip-pointed in Aunt Dee's direction.

Atim sighed. "If you need to carry anything, Aunt Dee, I have arms." The strongest of the Muskrats tried to make his voice sound cheerful. "I can meet these guys at the Station later."

Aunt Dee paused as she was about to get in. "Well... there is some stuff I'll need to put in the trunk. If you don't mind, I could use a younger set of hands."

Atim smiled and jogged over to the car. He waved at his cousins as Aunt Dee pulled out of the camp.

"Thank you." Brandon nodded at Chickadee as he rose to go check on his grandfather. "And tell Atim thank you when you see him."

The remaining Muskrats nodded, said their good-byes, and headed to the Station.

★

The heat of the sun had baked the inside of the car and it had the dusty smell of a vehicle that had spent a lot of time on the gravel roads that rolled through many First Nations. The inside of the car looked well lived in. Shirts and shoes spilled out of a small suitcase laid out over the back seat.

Atim found space for his feet on the floor between the disposable coffee cups, chocolate bar wrappers, and crumpled cellophane wrap. He watched the road, wracking his brain to come up with some suitable small talk. The silence escalated the quiet tension within the little car.

The temporary road leading out of the camp was soft and uneven, and Aunt Dee hit the bumps going at a good speed. The small car shook its passengers as its wheels plowed over the various potholes and bumps. When they leveled out, Aunt Dee and Atim were giggling from the tickles the rural rollercoaster had left in their tummies. The tension in the vehicle was gone.

"My grandpa was very happy to see you both." Atim smiled.

"He's an old friend. We've known him for ages. He knew my father."

"It was your father who gave you and Elder Leon the bundle?"

"Yes." Aunt Dee winced.

Atim cringed as he realized he had opened a wound that had just been briefly closed.

Aunt Dee noticed his discomfort and tapped him on the leg. "It's okay, my boy. The old lady isn't going to cry again." She laughed, and her eyes laughed too.

Atim suddenly understood how Chickadee had come to love this lady so quickly.

Aunt Dee sighed a sad sigh but she held a smile on her face.

In a few moments, they reached the arbor grounds and pulled up near the big teepee from Butterfly Narrows. They chatted about the Assembly as they made their way across the parking lot. Aunt Dee paused just inside the door to let her eyes adjust to the light filtering through the painted canvas. Then she crossed the space to a multi-colored star blanket that had been the site of the previous day's ceremony.

She kneeled down and began to fold the big quilt. "You know, my father hated TV. Movies too, really. He was old enough to call them both 'moving pictures.'" She chuckled. "He thought it was all fake, even the news. He said it was dangerous storytelling; filled our head with other people's ideas, and their pictures became our memories." She looked at Atim and smiled. Seeing that he was at a loss for something to do, she pointed to some bolts of cloth and jars sitting along the wall and the cardboard box beside them. Atim walked over and began filling the box.

"I think I know what your dad was talking about." Atim's right eye squinted as he thought. "I remember, when my grandmother was alive, she would tell me the story of *Goldilocks and the Three Bears*. I imagined what the bears looked like, they were fluffy and goofy, but still bears, you know?"

Aunt Dee nodded.

Atim reached back into his past with his left hand. "But then I saw a cartoon of the three bears, and after that, I could never see the bears the way I first imagined them. After that, I could only see the cartoon bears. Does that make sense?"

Aunt Dee assured him it did.

Atim shrugged. "It was weird."

"Yes. Imagine all the faces Cinderella had, given to her by all the children who heard her story over several generations. So many children probably gave her a face like their own. But now, she only has the face they remember from the movie."

"That's deep." Atim raised his eyebrows at the enormity of the thought.

"My father always said the power of the bundle was that it was evidence that the Cree Nation had a will of its own, the making of treaty." She stared into her memories as she spoke. "He always said there's power in the presence of history. And that's what people felt when they experienced the bundle. He made Leon and me promise we would never put the bundle on TV or take pictures of its contents. He said the bundle was a living thing and putting it in on film would be like drowning it in cement."

"Yeesh. That doesn't sound cool." With the box filled, Atim picked it up and joined Aunt Dee as she left the teepee carrying her folded blanket. When they reached the car, Aunt Dee popped the trunk.

Alongside a flat spare, a wrench, and a pint of open oil wrapped in rags, were garments and gear all in the Western style that the Shinning Deers seemed to love. Boxes of fringed frocks and footwear were squeezed in wherever they could fit. Atim found a low point in the array of items and set the box down within it.

Aunt Dee slammed the trunk and then put the blanket on the back seat. "Now, my boy, did you want me to take you somewhere?"

Atim shrugged. "No. I was going to catch up with my cousins. But thanks, Aunt Dee." He held out his arms to give her a hug.

With a willing smile, she wrapped her arms around him and squeezed tight. After holding him a moment, she pulled away, patted his biceps, and moved to open the door to the driver's seat. She didn't meet his eye as she spoke. "You're a good man, my boy." With that, she got into her little blue car and drove away.

CHAPTER 15

Dead Ends and Pink Locks

Walking on a shortcut through the bush, Chickadee, Otter, and Samuel were almost at the gas station when a jogging Atim caught up to them.

The Windy Lake gas depot was the last stop for a couple of hundred miles. It was always busy with the highway traffic flowing north and south. The locals called it the Station, but sometimes, especially in times like these, it was called the Drama Station.

The smell of greasy fries smacked the Muskrats in the nose as they opened the door to the Station's restaurant. Light streamed in from the large windows that overlooked the highway and gas pumps. The floor was tiled in blue squares offset with gray squares that could only reminisce about once being white. Empty seats far outnumbered those filled with customers. However, locals, travelers, and workers from the mine were scattered amongst the tables. An aged jukebox rocked old tunes in the corner.

"Is that Casey there?" Sam lip-pointed at a table in the corner. The leader of the teepee guards from Butterfly Narrows was eating lunch across from a young woman.

As the Muskrats walked toward the table, Casey noticed them. He nodded a welcome and stuck out his foot. "I got my runners back!"

"So, you talked to Uncle Levi?" Chickadee smiled at Casey and the woman with him.

"Yeah, I talked to him. Told him everything we knew."

"Even about Elder Lone Man going into the tent?" Samuel raised an eyebrow.

Casey hung his head for a moment. "Yes. Even that. We forgot about it the first time we spoke, but I'm sure Elder Lone Man didn't touch the bundle. He sure didn't come out with it, from what I saw."

"I don't think he did it either," Otter told Casey.

"Were there any times the guys from Butterfly Narrows all gathered together?" Sam kept up the probing.

"Once in the night and then in the morning when the hockey game downloaded. Late at night it was weird. One of the guys got all scared because he thought he heard a noise. We didn't hear anything. But we sure teased him about it." Casey and his girlfriend laughed.

"What do you think it was?" Chickadee asked.

"Don't know, really. He said it sounded like someone crying."

The girlfriend's ears pricked up. Her hair was cropped short on one side and hung long on the other. A streak of purple adorned the long side. "Must be a lot of people getting emotional. I saw an angry woman in the parking lot."

"There's so many people at the Assembly, I'm not surprised there was the occasional upset." Atim shrugged.

"Well, it might not have been crying. I didn't hear it, and my buddy wasn't too certain what he heard. Could have been a bird. Cat, maybe. Everyone was gone from the Assembly."

"So that was the only thing that was weird?" Sam asked.

Casey paused in thought for a moment and shook his head. "I can't think of anything else. If it would help your uncle, I'd tell him anything. I feel bad the bundle went missing under my watch."

"Really?" Atim sounded skeptical.

Casey looked him in the eye. "Man's word is important. I said I would protect the bundle…and it didn't work out that way. I want to see it returned too." His brow furrowed.

Atim nodded his understanding.

The Muskrats thanked Casey for talking with them and went into the convenience store area of the Station to discuss.

"One more suspect crossed off." Atim shook his head.

"Did we ever really suspect Casey?" Chickadee's eyebrow raised.

"Not really," Sam answered, "but I did want to talk to him about that night."

Otter threw up a hand. "Sooo, where to now?"

Sam sighed. "I don't know. We're waiting for Uncle to let us know if Guy was working the night the bundle went missing. And we still haven't talked to Pearl about anything."

"Well, let's hit the road." Sam was frustrated. "We're not getting anywhere here."

With the National Assembly of Cree Peoples in full swing, the roads of the rez were busier than usual. With no sidewalks, the Muskrats carefully walked along the shoulder of the road.

"You know…Uncle has removed all the crime scene tape from around the teepee." Otter watched his feet as he spoke.

"So?" Atim placed a hand on his little cousin's shoulder.

"Well, I'd like to look at the site too. And we can, now that he's done." Otter looked up at Atim.

"You think Uncle may have missed something?"

"Don't know. But, I want to check it out myself." The smallest Muskrat laughed.

"Well, we're running out of leads. The guards all seem to have their story together. I don't think Elder Lone Man did anything. He just isn't acting like he has a grudge that would push him to steal the bundle." Sam's face screwed up in consternation.

"So maybe it's time to look at other things." Atim raised his eyebrows.

The other Muskrats nodded in agreement.

"Yeah, but what?" asked Sam.

A crunch of gravel behind them announced that a vehicle had pulled over to the shoulder of the road. Turning around, the Muskrats watched their Uncle's band constable truck slowly roll to a stop. The driver's-side window whirred as it slid down.

"Hey Uncle! What's new?" Chickadee slapped the truck as she came up.

Uncle Levi took off his hat and scratched his sweaty head. "Some good news, I guess, if you like Guy."

The Muskrats looked at each other, not certain what to say.

Uncle Levi chuckled. "Nobody likes Guy, hey? Well, I called his boss. Turns out he was working the other night. So, it probably wasn't his cowboy boots making tracks in the teepee."

Sam groaned. "We're running out of things to check out!"

"This often happens in an investigation. You always get a lot of arrows pointing in different directions, but that doesn't mean they are pointing in the right way."

"So, what do you do when this happens?" Chickadee looked up at her uncle.

The big man shrugged and thought for a bit.

"Recheck the information, I guess. That's usually a good start. Often you've been told things that may reflect on other things…if you just look at them the right way." Uncle Levi let his hand float along the horizon as he spoke. "I got my own thinking to do about this, but I also have the usual day-to-day stuff to handle." He put his truck into gear. "Let me know if you see Pearl and her crew."

"It has to be them, Uncle." Atim stepped back away from the truck with the other Muskrats.

"We'll see." Uncle Levi grinned and drove away as the young sleuths watched.

"Guy isn't our guy." Atim flicked the hair out of eyes.

"I'm running out of ideas." Sam's shoulders slumped. "Maybe we just won't solve this one."

"Let's go check out the area around the teepee." Otter gave his cousin an encouraging shove.

★

"Who is that?" Atim was looking at a gaggle of youths from Windy Lake gathered around a tall, pink-haired teenager.

The Muskrats had quickly walked to the Assembly grounds, which were still teeming with Crees from far and wide, wandering through the displays, vendors, and food trucks—all doing their best to haggle cash out of them. The Muskrats were just passing the arbor when they saw the group of teens.

"Whoever it is has Bug hanging around." Sam stood on tiptoes as he walked so he could get a better view of the pink-haired girl.

"Is that...?" Chickadee's brows furrowed.

The girl suddenly started waving at the Muskrats. "Hey Chickadee! Chickadee!"

Chickadee's jaw dropped open. She shook her head and looked closely again. "Is that...?"

"It's Pearl!" Atim yelled and ran toward the group. He skidded to a stop just on the outside of their circle. The other Muskrats quickly joined him.

"Chickadee! Come here!" Pearl's voice was cheery.

The crowd parted and the new arrivals took a hesitant step forward.

Pearl twirled a pink lock between her fingers. "Did you see?"

The big teenager leaned forward and smiled freakishly wide as she showed the Muskrats her teeth.

"You have your braces, Pearl!" Atim slapped her on the arm.

The big girl laughed. "Yes! I feel so much better."

"Your hair is...pink...and the dark circles under your eyes are gone." Chickadee shook her head at the transformation.

"Yeah! Isn't it great? The other day, Ma got a call from my orthodontist. The government had finally given him permission to work on my teeth! Someone had canceled their appointment, so he offered it to me. That guy is super-busy and so is my ma. So it was a good score, after the long fight with those bureaucrats. We were just leaving when you saw us at the Station. Eddie wasn't too happy about it, but Ma made him take me." Pearl beamed. She took Chickadee by the arm and led her away from Bug and her other minions.

When Pearl and the Muskrats were a few steps away, she stopped and hung her head. "I want to apologize. I've been a jerk. I...I felt ugly with my teeth sticking out everywhere and scratching the inside of my cheek, and that made me do ugly things. I think I took that out on you. Especially you, Chickadee, 'cause you're cute and little and smart...all the things I wanted to be." Pearl sounded truly sorry.

Chickadee looked deep into Pearl's eyes and tried to glean her level of sincerity. "You've been so mean!" Chickadee wanted to hold back the tears, but her eyes glossed over, anyway.

"I know...but I promise, it'll be different from now on." The teenager took a step forward. "I don't care if you don't believe me now. I'll show you, I promise."

Chickadee was skeptical, but she imagined she could hear Grandpa's voice in her head, telling her to be kind and give Pearl another chance. "That would sure be nice. I will be watching."

Pearl smiled. "Thank you. I want to be…I'm going to be a different person."

Chickadee started to say something and then stopped.

Pearl reached out to her but didn't touch. "You can say whatever you're thinking."

Chickadee played with her fingers as she looked up at Pearl. "Could you be nicer to Bug? I think…he could be a different person too, if he thought more of himself, you know?"

A guilty frown shivered through Pearl's features. "Okay." She looked over at her cousin. Bug was being a jester, making a fool of himself, once again, to get people to like him. "He doesn't deserve…," Pearl trailed off sadly, aware of how her pain had flowed to others.

"I'm happy you're trying to change, Pearl." Chickadee reached out and pressed her bully's forearm.

The teenager shared her brace-filled grin with all the Muskrats. "I gotta go."

The four investigators stared after their former nemesis. Chickadee was super hopeful that the bully had turned over a new leaf.

"Well. That's terrible!!" Samuel threw up his hands.

The other Muskrats gave him a quizzical look.

"That was the last of our suspects," Sam explained.

"Now, we might as well be at step one. We got no more leads."

"There was never really any evidence that Pearl stole the bundle." Atim waggled his finger. The other three looked at him, incredulously.

"Uh…you just said 'It has to be them, Uncle!'" I didn't even want to mention Pearl to Uncle Levi. *You* did!" Sam smacked his brother on the shoulder.

Atim shrugged. "Water under the bridge."

Chickadee, Otter, and Sam shook their heads at the tallest Muskrat.

CHAPTER 16
Otter Tracks

Otter carefully studied the ground in front of him before he took another step forward. He had already checked out the earth around Elder Lone Man's teepee, but the crowds of people had wiped out any trace of the cowboy-boot tracks Uncle had mentioned.

Now Otter slowly looked for sign in the thin wind-break of trees and brush that ran near the backside of the teepee but stopped short before the large wooden arbor. The grass had grown longer within the trees. A blown chip bag, a chocolate bar wrapper, and other garbage was caught in its reedy web. The crowd of the Assembly muttered, laughed, and gossiped on either side of the tree divider.

In his mind's eye, Otter imagined the guards standing around the teepee the night before last. He could see Buckskin's spot, which would have been guarded throughout the darkness. Casey had been at the front. The guy that got scared would have been standing on this side of the teepee, watching the little strip of bush that Otter was now combing through.

There had always been trackers in Otter's family. He remembered, as a little boy, having a wolf track pointed out to him by his grandfather. The wolf's toes were well-defined, it was easy to imagine the size of the canine that pressed it into the once-wet soil. The old man had told him to watch the track, to keep an eye on it as it eroded and changed through time and weather. Otter had made a little fence of sticks around the wolf sign. He returned almost daily to visit the wild-crafted depression in the mud. He watched as the occasional rain softened it and summer's heat sucked out its moisture. Its edges crumbled, winter froze its withering, and spring's deluge eventually washed it away.

Otter smiled with pride. Tracking wasn't just the knowledge and experience of bushcraft, it was also about knowing hearts and minds. He took another slow step forward, patiently scanning the ground back and forth.

The children in the family had often been told about how Grandpa's late brother, Walter, known as the best tracker in the area, had found two little kids that had wandered off. For four days, police officers, volunteers, and, eventually, soldiers and helicopters had combed the area to no avail. Muttered whispers and furtive glances suggested fading hope that the children would be found. On the fourth day, Great-uncle Walter came in off the lake and was told of the missing children.

Otter grimaced. He knew the bush where the kids had been lost. The cold, gray spruce trunks were legion and marched off into the distance. The branches that held sharp, green needles were wide shoulders, high off the ground. A palisade of identical gray trunks would have met the children's gaze in every direction. The wind off the lake was cold there. The chilly humidity would have seeped through multiple layers of clothing. Otter shivered at the thought of being a small human spending one dark night, let alone three, in that harsh bit of forest.

After the soldiers, police, and volunteers had marched, shoulder to shoulder, through the brush, there was little sign of the missing children left upon the land. However, Great-uncle Walter found a one-inch fragment of a little girl's sweater in that swath of the great boreal forest and then, by thinking like a child, he was able to find the missing kids.

In describing their ordeal, the children said they soon realized they were lost and did their best to find their way home but eventually figured out they had been walking in the wrong direction. Spending a cold night among the gray sentinels of spruce, the youngsters had gone "bush crazy"—a great fear that the Elders say can overtake the lost, causing its victims to run from every noise they hear without judging whether it is friend or foe. Although, the children had heard the searchers, their irrational fear had caused them to flee their rescuers.

Great-uncle Walter's silent approach allowed him to find the bush-crazy kids, huddled together in the shadow of a large, cold stone they had been using as a windbreak.

"There is a sameness to the bush," Grandfather had told Otter as they sat on a rock looking over a stretch of wilderness. "It's almost like the static you see on TV, just a randomness, a scattering. So, when you are looking for something, look for difference, things that seem just a nudge off from the rest."

Another step forward. After looking for difference, Otter stood, put his hands on his hips, and leaned back to stretch out his spine. Returning his focus to the ground, the young tracker noticed a triangle of white dots nestled in the grass, just a few steps forward.

He quickly searched the ground in between, then took the two steps.

Three cigarette butts had fallen where someone had dropped them, their burnt ends pointing down. The grass right beside them had been tramped down, as though someone had stood on the spot for a while. Otter looked deeper, using his finger to trace out depressions partially obscured and altered by the foliage. While it wasn't the toe of a cowboy boot, a number of rounded squares, like the heel of a small boot, had been pressed into the earth.

★

"Looks like they came from the kind of thin cigarettes some women smoke." Samuel studied the butts now held in the palm of his hand.

"So, now we have a female suspect?" Chickadee's eyes widened.

"Looks like." Atim shook his head.

"From what Otter learned, it seems someone, possibly a woman, watched the guards for an opportune moment and then snuck in and stole the bundle," Samuel speculated.

"Remember when Uncle Levi said passion was a motivation for crime?" Chickadee looked around at her cousins.

"Maybe one of the guards' girlfriends wanted to make them look bad." Atim shrugged a shoulder.

"Did we see any of them smoke?" Sam looked around.

The cousins shook their heads.

"Smoking cigarettes is gross. Throwing your butts on the ground is the grossest part." Chickadee pretended to wretch.

"Really? I think it is that brown stain at the end. That's tar and chemicals and all sorts of stuff they put in the tobacco." Atim's nose wrinkled as he spoke.

"I hate it when I go into the bush and see cigarette butts and other garbage way back there. Makes me sad." Otter frowned.

Atim chuckled and slapped Otter on the shoulder. "You know, I heard a news story on the radio that said sitting is the new smoking. Sitting around all the time is the next unhealthy habit."

"Everyone should pick up their butts, I guess," Otter said with a little wonder in his voice. The other Muskrats laughed.

Otter squinted and scratched the back of his head. "I have to go home. It's getting late. Grandpa is going to have a pipe ceremony with the Elders from Butterfly Narrows tomorrow morning. Sort of a unity thing." He stood on his tiptoes to get a view of the arbor.

The Muskrats began to head out of the Assembly grounds and toward home.

"Remember how the scared guy thought he heard crying?" Sam's thoughts were focused on the case. "Maybe we should be looking for a sad woman."

"Tears can be angry." Chickadee watched her feet as she spoke. "Maybe if we walk around the Assembly during the unity ceremony, we could find someone who is emotional about something." There was an edge of skepticism in her voice.

"We could check out the crowd while Otter helps Grandpa," Atim said to Sam and Chickadee. With a flick of his head, he tossed the hair out of his eyes. "Looks like revenge is back on the table."

CHAPTER 17
Bundle-bound

"A nation is not a group of people who agree with one another." Grandpa waved his arms over the crowd as he spoke. "We know the lessons of Creation are in our lands, and the Cree people are spread across many different teachings, so it is not surprising that the things we think and do are touched by different beliefs and histories and needs and stories and wants."

"My friend speaks the truth." Elder Lone Man held out his hand to the Muskrats' grandfather.

Grandpa echoed the gesture by grasping his new ally's forearm.

Elder Lone Man's wide smile flashed. "We had a disagreement and we allowed the words spoken to stand, when we could have let them flow past. And so, we both had to overcome that. We had to remember we are Cree, and love one another, even if we have disagreements."

A lump rose in Otter's throat as he listened to the two Elders. From his spot as an Elder's helper, he looked around at the group assembled in the arbor. The majority of those gathered sat under the wide circle of shade made by the arbor's roof of spruce boughs and shingled plywood. Sam and Atim were fidgeting a few sections of wooden bleachers away from the V.I.P.s. Chickadee was with the older women, hair neatly braided, a bright smile on her face, her hand clasped in Aunt Dee's.

Otter looked around the ceremonial circle. Children laughed and ran, dodging adults and engaging in their own world. Women in lawn chairs were sewing some items to sell during the Christmas season, others to keep their own family warm through the approaching winter. Brown, old men listened attentively to the speakers, oblivious to the hubbub around them but still open to the occasional joke from the buddy beside them. And women Elders sat quietly, nodding along with what they agreed with, their thumbs circling around each other in a forever twiddle.

While Grandpa and Elder Lone Man spoke of the diversity among the Cree people, the people themselves felt the similar feelings and teachings that existed within their beings. Otter smiled at the wonder of Creation that both similarities and differences could be true at the same time.

Under his battered red-and-white baseball cap, Elder Lone Man smiled wide. "Long ago, disputes were almost always resolved through ceremony. As the Nehiyew, we have to bring back the old laws, and that includes the ways we used to bring our arguments to an end, not only among our family and other families, but at the community-to-community level, too."

Grandpa was wearing an old brain-tanned and beaded jacket that his late wife had made for him long ago. Dark green and light green triangles on a strip of white beads stretched down each side of his chest. Otter knew it was like a protective cloak for his Elder, a garment that swathed him in memories of love and family. It lent the old man strength.

"We have to remember that our grandfathers and their grandfathers were people, so, occasionally there were arguments and thefts and even murders." Grandpa raised an eyebrow as he looked over the crowd. "And, if that's true, why should we be proud of them?" He paused to let the question sink in before answering it. "Because the good people came together and dealt with the unhealthy, the lonely, and the hurt among them. And they came together to create laws that helped settle feuds and dealt with wrong-doing."

Elder Lone Man's huge spectacles glinted in the sunlight. He was obviously happy in his jeans, bush jacket, and cap. "With their laws, our ancestors survived the cold of our winters, the heat of our summers, and through the many generations that led to us." Elder Lone Man gestured to the crowd.

Grandpa nodded and continued. "We are a strong people. Stronger still, when we think of each other and work together. We see this in our treaty-making. While the Crown's negotiators thought of the wants of that day's masters, our ancestors were thinking of their next Seven Generations. Linking us all, not only through shared lands, but also time itself."

The Muskrats' grandfather stretched his hand out to his friend Elder Shining Deer. "I want to thank Elder Leon for bringing the Treaty 12 Bundle."

Otter noticed Elder Leon for the first time. The man had shrunk. He sat in a dark blue windbreaker, and his hair was disheveled.

Grandpa's brow grew stern as he spoke. "A terrible thing has happened…but when terrible things happen, the people must go on. We must continue paddling our families, our Nation, forward. So, we will have a pipe ceremony to bring us all together." He looked back at Elder Leon. "Of course, we thank you, my friend, for bringing us the Treaty 12 Bundle—such a powerful symbol of unity. We all hope for its return. Did you want to say some words, Leon?"

The former Bundle Holder blinked, pursed his lips, and then shook his head. He held out his hands and mouthed *thank you* and *sorry* to his friend, but Elder Leon was obviously not in a state to speak.

The Muskrats' grandfather frowned in sympathy and gave one quick nod to his grieving friend.

*

As Grandpa mentioned Elder Leon, Aunt Dee's grip tightened on Chickadee's hand, while her free fingers rushed to her face to stifle a gasp.

Aunt Dee still looked great, her hair was sculpted, and she sat in a dark blue, white, and turquoise ribbon skirt that stretched down to the ground. A matching purse rested on the ground between them. But Chickadee was worried about her new Elder. It was obvious she was distraught. The young sleuth figured it was natural for a couple to be upset when part of their lives was missing.

But as Elder Leon declined the invitation to speak, Aunt Dee sobbed. Chickadee watched as she continued to fuss. Aunt Dee sighed and tried to hold back the tears. She flipped open her purse, pulled a tissue out, and wiped her eyes.

Chickadee turned to her. "Do you want to step outside the ceremony for a moment, Aunt Dee?"

The older woman nodded and rose, and with head bowed and a tissue covering her face, she quickly left the teepee. Chickadee followed in her wake.

Outside, Aunt Dee made a beeline for an empty picnic table. She plopped down hard.

For the first time, Chickadee realized there was anger mixed in with her Elder's sorrow.

They sat quietly there for a few minutes. Eventually, Aunt Dee urged Chickadee to go back to the ceremony and leave her to collect herself.

Still concerned, Chickadee didn't want to abandon her friend, but the older woman insisted on some time alone. With a soft good-bye, Chickadee left.

On her way back to arbor, she ran into Atim and Sam standing on the edge of the circle.

"I think there is something wrong with Aunt Dee." Chickadee looked back across the field at the older woman.

"Well, they're obviously upset about the bundle being missing," Sam said with a shrug.

"It's more than that...." Atim looked concerned. "When we were in the car, she suddenly started talking about her dad and TV. Came out of nowhere. Kind of weird and sad all at the same time...."

Suddenly, like a bolt of lightning, a memory flowed through Atim. In a flash, his long legs were carrying him swiftly toward Aunt Dee. His brother and cousin, taken by surprise, watched him run off with their mouths open.

Slowing to a stop before his Elder, Atim suddenly realized he had no idea how to ask what he wanted.

Aunt Dee looked up at him expectantly.

"Do you have a light, Aunt Dee?"

She gave him a quizzical look, but her face quickly

changed to chagrin. "I do. When I get stressed, I smoke cigarettes. It's a weakness." She reached into her purse and pulled out a small pack of cigarettes—the thin kind. Atim could see they ended like the butts Otter found near the big teepee.

She held the lighter out to Atim.

He shook his head. "Aunt Dee, when I put the blanket in the trunk, I noticed you had cowboy boots…."

A confused expression flitted across her face. "Yes, I wear them in the evenings, when the ground gets too cold or damp for moccasins."

Atim pressed his lips together and flicked the hair out of his eyes. Quietly, he asked, "Aunt Dee…did *you* take the bundle?"

Mrs. Shining Deer gasped, sat up straight, and looked Atim in the eye. The anger was gone now, and sorrow-filled tears spilled over her elderly face. She took the young sleuth's hands in her own.

Aunt Dee leaned forward, she whispered. "Yes! My husband broke his promise."

CHAPTER 18
Pride Before Fault

"It was only phone texts, Grandpa." Atim shrugged a shoulder as he spoke. "Is it really that big a deal?"

Grandpa gave his grandson a hard look, his face dark, brow furrowed, and lips pressed together.

After hearing Aunt Dee's story from Atim, as a group, the Muskrats decided to speak to Grandpa to figure out the correct steps to take next. The responsibility given by the new information weighed heavily on the investigators. Not only was Aunt Dee's heart broken, but there were the people of Treaty 12 and the entire Cree Nation to consider.

Atim remembered the mix of pain and anger in Aunt Dee's voice as she told her story. While taking pictures on her husband's phone during the bundle's welcoming ceremony, a text came through. Looking further, Aunt Dee found a whole conversation. She learned her husband had been communicating with a reality TV producer who wanted to do a show centered around Elder Leon's travels and teachings with the Treaty 12 Bundle. Aunt Dee had explained that the producer had approached them many times before about doing a show on the bundle, but as a couple, they had always refused. But this time, the producer approached the Bundle Holder alone, without Aunt Dee, and had returned with a show focused on Elder Leon. Elder Leon had gone behind his wife's back and had agreed to be a part of the show. Aunt Dee's pain over the betrayal was soul-shattering. Her sobs had been drawn from her whole being.

Atim looked over Windy Lake as he thought. The water lapped at a rough patch of shore that was down the hill and across a gravel lane from Grandpa's yard. The wind chopped the waves into frothy slices. The Muskrats convened around the unlit firepit that was the gathering place of so many large family assemblies too big or celebratory to fit in Grandpa's little house.

Grandpa had been upset ever since the Muskrats told him. He rarely showed anger, but his tense silence after he'd been told was uncomfortable.

The old man sat on one of the stumps—the only furniture in the meeting space. "The Speaker inside us, stands right beside our Decider. Our communication, no matter whether we lie or not, comes from our center, our soul. When we stray from the truth of our lives, we create blockages and...whirlpools within ourselves that distort and tarnish. A man with the duty that Elder Shining Deer has, holds a sacred trust to his community, to the people of his treaty area. And to the vows he made to his mentor and teacher, as well as his wife."

Atim sat on a stump across the cold firepit from his grandfather. "But Grandpa, his teacher is dead.... And even Aunt Dee says she'll forgive him if he doesn't do the show."

Grandpa scoffed. "The honor of keeping the promise has nothing to do with the breathing-status of Aunt Dee's father. But it has everything to do with the level of honor Leon was holding himself to. He let his pride get the better of him, and it was his pride that caused him to distort the truth to his wife. When you walk a spiritual road, the snare of pride presents itself every morning. Pride isn't a test that needs to be passed just once."

Sam paced as he listened, but, eventually, a torrent of questions spilled out. "Okay. Aunt Dee took the bundle. So, was it really stolen? If so, does this mean the case of the burgled bundle is solved? Do we tell Uncle Levi? If not, what happens next?"

Grandpa looked up at the sky as he processed the flow of inquiry. "No. Kind of. Yes. Finding the bundle was an important step, but how the bundle is returned to the circle is just as important."

Chickadee's ears pricked up when she heard he grandfather's response. "So, Aunt Dee isn't in trouble?"

The Muskrats' Elder shook his silver mane. "She shouldn't be. Back when we governed ourselves, the women were the conscience of our Nations. It was their duty to judge whether the leadership was being honorable and putting the people's survival before their own desires. Your Aunt Dee was also given a responsibility to care for and honor the bundle. She was just fulfilling her role as a protector of the bundle."

Chickadee clasped her hands excitedly, and Atim breathed a sigh of relief.

Otter sat beside his grandfather. "Brandon always said that Aunt Dee's feelings about the bundle were all wrapped up in their promise to her father."

"The oath to keep the bundle is separate from marriage vows, but both are connected to the honor of the people making the promises." Grandpa's flat hand cut a swath through the air.

Chickadee smiled. "I like the idea of the women being the inner guide to the people."

Grandpa grinned back. "When you're living close to the earth, survival of everyone is important for the future of the people as a people. It was the women, our water-carriers and life-givers, who were most tuned in to the health of the young and old. They were the best judges of how well the leader was doing."

Samuel had continued to pace. His backlog of questions had been building.

Grandpa looked over his shoulder at his grandson. "You get one question."

Sam's eyebrows shot up, he sucked in his breath, and then blew it out. "Uh...." Sam's face looked like he was trying to push something out of his body.

His brother and cousins hardly tried to hide their snickering.

Finally, Sam sighed. "I guess...what do we do now?"

Grandpa laughed and rubbed his chin. "Nothing!"

The Muskrats' shoulders slumped.

Their grandfather put a hand on Atim's shoulder as he looked around at them. "There are some things that even the Mighty Muskrats have to leave to us adults. I will discuss this with Dee, and then Leon, and we'll figure something out. The bundle must be returned to the circle in a good way. And it has to be done before the Assembly breaks."

CHAPTER 19

Case Closed, Bundle Opened

The Treaty 12 Bundle was the center of a ceremony being witnessed by the many families gathered in the Windy Lake arbor at the National Assembly of Cree Peoples. Brandon Shining Deer was on his knees before the sacred package, preparing for the protocols around unwrapping, then rewrapping, the memory bundle.

Earlier, quilts had been placed on the ground by the Elders' helpers.

Now, the old men sat on the star blanket in the center. Otter and Cree First Nations youth, from James Bay to the Rocky Mountains, filled their Elder's pipes and then passed them over.

Samuel watched from his place on the bleachers. He had admitted to both himself and his cousins that he was a little jealous of Otter's knowledge of ceremony.

"The bundle was not lost!" Grandpa grinned as he

spoke to the crowd. "The bundle was just telling us that it was time for it to move on, time for a new generation to take over." He gestured toward Elder Leon and Aunt Dee.

They were sitting together in the front row, on fold-out chairs, their hands locked together. They nodded as Grandpa smiled at them.

"We are seeing something special today. My friend Leon is passing the bundle on to his grandson, Brandon. Which means, Elder Shining Deer has something to say." Grandpa sat down on the nearest corner of a bleacher as his friend rose to speak.

"Thank you to my friend. Windy Lake is a beautiful place with beautiful people." Elder Leon's composure was back. His hair was neatly combed, and his clothes once again matched his wife's. "Normally, this ceremony would happen on the sacred places of Treaty 12. But sometimes the bundle speaks, and then those who guard the honor of the bundle will say it is time." Elder Leon smiled at his wife. He paused and stared at the ground, then let out a lungful of air. "I have enjoyed being the caretaker for the bundle. Maybe, I enjoyed it too much. I let the honor of that position go to my head. I got…," he held his hands on either side of his ears, "big-headed." His chuckle was sad. "But I am proud of my grandson and the man he has become and the work he has done to learn how to carry the weight of the bundle. He has been working hard to learn the protocols that go along with the bundle, to learn the stories and be fluent in his language, so he can tell the stories as they are meant to be told. And he knows to listen to the stories of other families, so he can find the knowledge he doesn't hold. With so many of us searching, I think it is a good time to give the bundle to someone who has the strength of youth, the voice of the young people."

Chickadee watched Aunt Dee's face. There was still sadness there, but there was also hope. Grandpa and the Shining Deers seemed relieved after their discussion on how to move forward.

"It was through ceremony that many disputes were resolved. But also, how things were passed on. We smoke the long pipe because we believe the smoke will carry our intentions skyward, and all of Creation will share the true reflections of our hearts. I will smoke the pipe with my grandson now and he will become bound by his promise before you all."

The older and the younger man sat across from each other, the bundle on one side, and they passed the pipe back and forth. Aunt Dee joined them, and she touched the pipe during the ceremony, signifying her consent for the transfer of responsibilities.

After the ceremony, Brandon and the Elders gave the crowd a break, asking them to return in fifteen minutes.

The Muskrats gathered near the Elders and waited to speak to the Shining Deers. Brandon was the first to notice them and walked over. He took Chickadee's hands in his own and then shook hands with each of the boys. "I want to thank you for finding the bundle, even if it wasn't lost." He laughed. "My grandfather and grandmother are no longer arguing. I think she is relieved that all the moving and costs and protocols of keeping the memory bundle are moving on to me." The new Bundle Holder rubbed the back of his neck. "They never said why they decided to do this now. But, I guess, that is between them." He shrugged.

Otter slapped his new mentor on the arm. "You'll be great at taking care of the bundle and its stories."

"Well, this will be my first time leading the unpacking and then repacking of the bundle. It is up to me how to tell the story of the bundle moving to a new keeper."

The Muskrats were impressed.

Brandon waved off their gushing. "Can you do me a favor? Can you think of something small that would represent you all? I'd like to make it part of a gift."

"For your grandparents? Of course! We'd love to give them a memento of us," Chickadee told him. The boys agreed.

"Make sure it's something small. I'll come get it off you later." Brandon grinned and waved as he walked away.

The young sleuths could see their grandpa was alone for a moment and they ran to him, eager to get more news about how the bundle was actually found.

Chickadee, Atim, and Otter pushed Sam forward to ask the questions.

"Hey Grandpa. It's pretty cool that the bundle is being passed to Brandon." Sam smiled at his grandfather as the old man rested on a chair.

"Yes. Very cool." The old man grinned, knowing he had information the Muskrats wanted.

"Are you going to tell us, Grandpa?" Chickadee grabbed a foldout chair and sat down beside him.

"All right, Muskrats." Their Elder chuckled. "Well... Aunt Dee has forgiven Leon for his poor choices. Now, it is up to him to earn back the trust of his wife. But Elder Leon cannot earn forgiveness from Dee's father. The man he gave his word to has already crossed over, so it was thought... it would be best if the bundle moved on."

Sam's eyes grew big. "But where *was* the bundle, Grandpa?"

"Did you see the little teepee at the Shining Deer camp?"

The Muskrats nodded.

"Well, that's where they usually keep it when they are away from home. Aunt Dee dug a hole under the blanket the bundle is usually placed upon and buried it there. Our focus was on the big tent, not the little one." Grandpa chuckled at the thought.

Otter smiled. "So now it's returning to the circle in a good way?"

Grandpa looked around at the young sleuths. "As you know, Brandon has always been a caring student. He is devoted to his teachings...and his grandparents. They will watch over him as he takes on the role of Bundle Holder and Knowledge Keeper." The old man groaned as he stood. Otter gave his grandfather a shoulder to lean on.

Sam and Atim followed their grandfather as he continued to speak about Brandon's new responsibilities.

Chickadee and Atim noticed that the crowds of well-wishers had passed on, and Aunt Dee now stood alone. They took the moment to skip over. Chickadee took her new Elder's hand. "Is everything all right, Aunt Dee?" A huge smile launched itself from Chickadee's pudgy cheeks.

The old lady smiled down at them. "It's getting better. Thanks to you Muskrats." She grinned at Atim and patted Chickadee's hand. "I'm not sure I would have come out with it, if Atim hadn't asked the question. I was so thankful when your grandfather approached us in the morning."

"You were not angry that we...told him about you?" Chickadee's brow furrowed.

Aunt Dee hugged her. "No. You told someone who really cares about us that we needed help. I cannot fault you for that." After the embrace, she met Chickadee's eyes with a twinkle in her own. "But I hope, now that you know our secret, the Muskrats will keep it to themselves. It is so much harder to heal when people are gossiping."

"I promise, Aunt Dee." Atim gave her a hug as well.

"And I'm pretty certain the boys won't think about this again, once we're on to the next case," Chickadee assured her.

Aunt Dee was thoughtful for a moment. She looked at her hands. "I could have done things better. But I didn't know what to do."

Atim shook his head. "You don't have to explain, Aunt Dee. You were caught in a tough place."

The old woman stared at her husband, who was talking to someone nearby.

Mrs. Shining Deer shook her head. "He's a good man, you know. He's just…always pushing, always wanting more. He says he'll make it up to me, earn back my trust, and I believe him."

Chickadee shrugged. "Boys are yucky."

Aunt Dee laughed, gave Chickadee one last embrace and then gently pushed her and Atim back toward Grandpa and the other Muskrats. The heaviness of their conversation hadn't let them walk too far away.

When the four of them were back together, the Muskrats' thoughts turned to Brandon's request.

"We need something quick." Sam snapped his fingers.

"Something small…that represents us." Otter looked thoughtful.

Chickadee pointed to a large sitting-stump. "Here! Empty your pockets. Let's see what we got!"

The boys dumped the trinkets, treasures, and trash they had been carrying around with them on to the large, round slice of wood.

Otter threw down a guitar pick and a flat, reddish rock. Atim had been carrying a wrench, a screw, and a few empty Hot Rod wrappers. Sam had a deck of cards and his house keys, which tinkled on a keychain from the Windy Lake gas station.

After the boys unloaded, Chickadee's pockets held the USB stick that connected her to Wi-Fi and the K button from the keyboard in the Muskrats' fort.

"Yeesh! Just a lot of junk." Atim tossed the hair out of his eyes and slapped his forehead.

"He said it would be part of a gift, so it's not the whole thing, he just needs a small reminder of us." Chickadee rubbed the tallest Muskrat's shoulder. "Brandon is probably sticking it to a card or something for his grandparents."

She picked up the USB stick. "Well, I'm not giving this." She returned Atim's screw, wrench, and spicy, pepperoni stick wrappers. "These are no good for a card. Neither are these." She tossed Sam his deck. She picked up the K key. "This would only be helpful if they were the Skinning Deers," she snickered.

"Ever gruesome!" Otter shook his head.

"Whatever, Elvis. Here's your guitar pick." Chickadee held out the tiny piece of plastic.

That left the Windy Lake keychain and the flat, reddish rock.

Samuel picked up the keychain and started removing his keys.

Chickadee picked up the rock. "This from Pebble Beach?"

Otter nodded.

The mention brought back a flood of memories for each of the Muskrats. Pebble Beach was where the family pulled up their canoes when they were heading to Grandma's favorite berry-picking spot.

It was really a beach in the making. The work of rolling water over a few hundreds of thousands of years had shattered the limestone shore into a scattering of millions of red, reddish, rose, white, off-white, light brown, beige, and creamy coffee-colored rocks that tinkled when the waves washed over them. While their colors were diverse, they were all fairly uniform in shape: thin, smooth on both sides, and about the size of a small cookie. For over two miles, the fifteen feet between the bush and the lake was filled with nature's most perfect skipping stones.

The Muskrats were all captured by their many memories of that place. It was one of the most picturesque locations along Windy Lake.

"Keep your keys on, Smarty Pants." Chickadee looked at Samuel as she waved the rock around in front of the boys. "We're going with the rock."

With chuckles, the Mighty Muskrats were all in agreement.

Atim looked up at the cloudless sky. "It's sooo nice out."

Sam smiled and skipped a few steps. "I feel good too."

Chickadee, grinning, teased her cousins. "A little bit of Cree pride, and you boys are all fired up."

Her cousins laughed.

"Guess so." Otter shrugged.

"It's a good thing." Atim nodded.

★

A few minutes later, the stone memento was with Brandon, and the Muskrats were once again in the ceremony. Atim, Chickadee, and Sam tried their best to listen from the bleachers, occasionally lapsing into poking and teasing one another until they earned a chastising look from a nearby Elder. Otter was posted beside his grandfather, prepared to do whatever protocols required.

The bundle sat on a blanket. It looked like a watermelon-sized pill. The outside wrapping was a piece of well-worn teepee canvas. Straps of the rough material bound it tightly into its oval shape, and strips of multicolored prayer ties, attached to and around the bundle, completed its decoration.

It doesn't look like much, Sam thought.

The ceremony to open the memory pack took time as Brandon had to reintroduce everything wrapped in the bundle back to this world. The layers of different-colored cloth each held items that were packed with meaning, talismans of memories, and stories that stretched back generations.

During the opening, the pipes were smoked. The fire bowls' breath was used to cleanse and carry skyward the intentions of the participants throughout the protocols.

Eventually, the Treaty 12 Bundle was fully exposed. Everything that had been a part of the memory capsule; the items from the long-ago treaty-making and the items it had picked up along its journey to the present day, were all laid out on the blankets. They were surrounded by the many different-colored cloths that had made up the layers of the packaged memory.

When the bundle opening was over, Brandon stood and began to speak to the crowd. Although, this was his first time leading the ceremony, it was obvious he was comfortable speaking in front of a group.

"Now, everyone will get a chance to walk by the open bundle and see what was inside. But before we do that, I want to bring up four young people who helped my family bring the bundle back into the Circle of the Cree Nation and back into the Circle of the People of Treaty 12, once we get it back home." Brandon stretched out a hand to the Muskrats on the bleachers, and then one out to Otter by the Pipe Carriers. "Atim, Chickadee, Sam... and Otter please come up and stand by my family and the bundle." He pointed to a spot at the front of the crowd. "We see bundles as living things, so we want you to stand as honored guests of the Treaty 12 Bundle itself."

The Muskrats looked at each other. They stood and slowly walked to the place Brandon indicated. Once there, Brandon smiled at them and continued to talk. "Please, let's all line up. And then everyone can come and experience the items that were a part of the making of Treaty 12. As you do, remember the vision of our ancestors as they tried to make an agreement that met *our* needs, so many generations in the future. And don't forget to say hello to the bundle's honored guests, the Mighty Muskrats!!"

The assembled all queued up and began to shamble past the sacred items from Treaty 12. The Elders, being at the front, were the first to mosey past the bundle, shake the Muskrats' hands, smile out a quip or comment, and then shuffle out of the teepee. After Grandpa had filled him in, Uncle Levi came through the line, congratulated them, shook their hands, gave Chickadee a hug, and slapped each of the boys on the back. Denice and the aunties also made a show of how proud they were of the young investigators. With so many well-wishers, it took some time for the entire crowd to go through.

After they shook hands and gave out hugs, Atim looked over at the contents of the treaty bundle laid out on the blanket. "It doesn't look like much," he whispered at his cousins.

"What did you expect? A unicorn's head?" Chickadee hissed, annoyed at his irreverence.

Atim snickered. "Bigfoot's foot, maybe."

"I think it's cool. Like a museum exhibit of our history, you know. Not Canadian or European history, but *our* history," Samuel said quietly, as he tried to memorize the shape and color of each item he saw.

"Well…the treaty was made with the Crown." Atim was happy to be able to remind his brother of a detail.

Sam rolled his eyes. "Yeah, but…this is *our* law. The Treaty 12 people's side of the story. You know how Americans love their constitution. I think they have it framed someplace."

Chickadee, Otter, and Atim nodded.

"This isn't our constitution, but it's just as important to our people. Remember when Grandpa talked about how we're all citizens of different layers? Our family, our town, our Nation?" Sam paused and looked at his brother. "Well, this is important on a higher level than us."

Atim looked back at the items spread out on the blanket and reconsidered their importance. He knew that each inspired a story, a snapshot of history that the Treaty 12 Elders from long ago had decided the people needed to keep. Brandon had told them the storytelling that went with the bundle would start in the morning and go for the next three days.

When everyone sat back down, Brandon rose again to speak. He held his hand up to gather the attention of the National Assembly of Cree Peoples.

"It is our way to reward those who have done good work for the community. I asked these four young people to provide a small token that represented them. They gave me this rock." The young Bundle Holder held up the flat, round, limestone disk that Otter had given him earlier. "They told me it reminded them of the special places that make up Windy Lake."

The local people in the crowd nodded and smiled. They all recognized a stone from Pebble Beach, a place whose beauty inspired many wonderful memories in everyone.

Brandon held a hand out toward the Muskrats, his smile filled with gratitude. "And isn't it like them? When I mentioned I needed something small for a gift, they assumed that gift was for someone else. But no…."

Aunt Dee clapped with excitement. She was obviously aware of what Brandon was about to say.

Brandon turned the rock over in his hands as he spoke. "Over the next few days, I will begin to rewrap the bundle, and as each piece is reentered and a new layer of colored cloth added, another story will be told. The closer to the center, the older the story." The young man smiled at the crowd. It was obvious they enjoyed listening to him.

Samuel grinned as he remembered being told that the Cree people always valued a good storyteller. The young Bundle Holder was sure to make his family proud.

Brandon's gestures were quick and sharp, adding strength to his words. "As the new Bundle Holder, I can add my own experience, and the first item I will add will be this flat, red stone from Windy Lake, and it will remind me to tell the story of how the bundle spoke through the investigations of the Mighty Muskrats! This is my gift to them, for the gift they have given myself, my family, and all the people of Treaty 12!!" Brandon ended with a shout and spread his arms wide. He indicated the Muskrats should stand. Bashfully, the Muskrats stood and smiled back at the now-clapping, hooting, and hollering Neechies gathered from across the wide and diverse breadth of the Cree Nation.

Author's Note

I wanted to add a short word about some of the choices I made while writing *The Mighty Muskrats and the Case of the Burgled Bundle*.

First, I did not go into great detail describing the steps within the ceremonies, the contents of the bundle, or the actual delivery of oral history because of the philosophy described within the pages of the book. An Elder within *Burgled Bundle* says, "It is the experience that is the message."

Second, just as the Windy Lake First Nation is a fictional community, so too is Treaty #12 a fictional treaty area. The Numbered Treaties currently end with Treaty #11. I chose to do this because there are actual Bundle Holders in many treaty areas, and I did not want my story to reflect on these Knowledge Keepers and their important work.

Thank you for meeting the Mighty Muskrats.

I hope you will continue to explore Windy Lake with them.

ABOUT THE AUTHOR

MICHAEL HUTCHINSON is a citizen of the Misipawistik Cree Nation in the Treaty 5 territory, north of Winnipeg. As a teen, he pulled nets on Lake Winnipeg, fought forest fires in the Canadian Shield, and worked at the Whiteshell Nuclear Research Station's Underground Research Lab. As a young adult, he worked as a bartender, a caterer for rock concerts and movie shoots, and, eventually, as a print reporter for publications such as *The Calgary Straight* and *Aboriginal Times*. After being headhunted by the Indian Claims Commission, Michael moved from journalism to the communications side of the desk and worked for the ICC in Ottawa as a writer. He returned to his home province to start a family. Since then, he has worked as the Director of Communications for the Assembly of Manitoba Chiefs, and as a project manager for the Treaty Relations Commission of Manitoba, where he helped create the "We are all treaty people" campaign. Over seven years ago, he jumped at the chance to make mini-documentaries for the first season of *APTN Investigates*. Michael then became host of APTN National News and produced APTN's sit-down interview show, *Face to Face*, and APTN's version of *Politically Incorrect*, *The Laughing Drum*. Michael was recently in charge of communications for the Manitoba Keewatinowi Okimakanak, an advocacy organization for First Nations in northern Manitoba. He currently lives in Ottawa, Ontario where he continues to advocate for First Nation families and communities across Canada. His greatest accomplishments are his two lovely daughters.

LOOK FOR THE NEXT BOOK IN
THE MIGHTY MUSKRATS MYSTERY SERIES

THE CASE OF
THE RIGGED
RACE

IN SPRING 2022